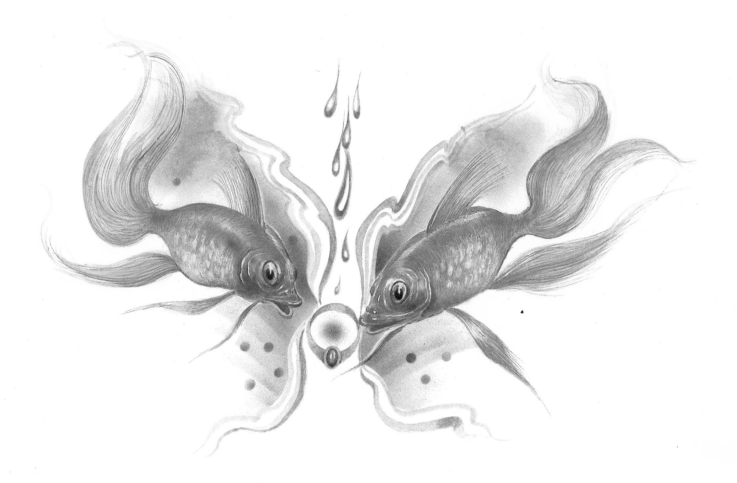

Stories selection: VIERA JANUSOVÁ
Illustrations: ALEXEJ VOJTÁŠEK

Designed by ONDREJ MÁRIÁSSY
Translation: HEATHER TREBATICKÁ

Copyright © 1988 Slovart Publishers, Bratislava
English Language Edition designed and produced by
Autumn Publishing Limited, Chichester, England

This 1988 edition published by Derrydale Books,
distributed by Crown Publishers, Inc.,
225 Park Avenue South
New York
New York 10003

Typeset by The Graphic Image, Hampshire, England
Printed in Czechoslovakia

ISBN 0 517 64983 7
h g f e d c b a

25 FAIRY TALES and FABLES

25 FAIRY TALES and FABLES

DERRYDALE BOOKS
New York

Contents

The brave
tin soldier

There were once 25 tin soldiers. They were all brothers as they had been made out of one old piece of tin. They held muskets in their hands, looked straight ahead and had beautiful red and blue uniforms. The first thing they heard when the lid was taken off their box, was "Tin soldiers!" Those were the words of a little boy who clapped his hands in delight. He had been given them for his birthday and now he set them out on the table. The soldiers were all exactly alike, except one, which was a little different from the rest. He had only one leg, because he was the last one to be made and there had not been enough tin left. However, he stood on his one leg as firmly as the others stood on two. It was this soldier that had a remarkable adventure.

On the table where the boy had set out the soldiers there were a lot of other toys. The one that attracted most attention was a pretty cardboard castle. Through the little windows you could see straight into the hall. In front of the castle there were some tiny trees arranged around a little mirror, which looked like a lake. Plastic swans were swimming on it. It was all very beautiful, but the most beautiful of all was the little doll in the doorway of the castle. She was also cut out of cardboard, but her skirt was made of the finest muslin and a narrow blue ribbon was draped across her shoulders and fastened with a brooch as big as her face. The doll was standing with outstretched arms because she was a dancer. She held one of her legs so high that it disappeared under her skirt and the tin soldier could not see it. He thought that, like himself, she had only one leg.

"That would be just the wife for me!" he thought. "But she is

very noble, after all she lives in a castle and I have only a box which is no place for her. I must try to get to know her!" Then he lay down behind a snuff-box that was on the table. From there he had the best view of the dainty little lady who remained standing on one leg without losing her balance.

When evening came, all the other tin soldiers were put away in their box and the people who lived in the house went to bed. Now all the toys began to play. They would visit each other, fight battles and give parties. The tin soldiers rattled around in their box. They wanted to play, too, but they could not lift off the lid. The nut-crackers turned somersaults and the pencil danced over the blackboard. There was such a din that the canary woke up and began talking to them. The only two who did not move were the tin soldier and the little dancer. She balanced on the point of her foot, with her arms outstretched in front of her, and the soldier stood as enduringly on his one foot. He did not turn his eyes away from the dancer for even a second.

Twelve o'clock struck. Snap! The lid of the snuff-box sprang open. But there was no snuff inside, only a little black goblin. You see, it was a Jack-in-the-box.

10

"Tin soldier!" said the goblin. "Keep your eyes to yourself!"
But the tin soldier pretended he had not heard.
"You just wait until tomorrow!" said the goblin.
In the morning, when the children got up, they put the tin soldier on the window ledge. The window suddenly flew open and the tin soldier fell out head first from the third floor. It was a terrible fall; he turned upside down with his leg in the air and helmet downwards, and when he hit the ground his bayonet got stuck between two paving stones.

A servant girl immediately ran downstairs with the little boy to look for the soldier. But even though they very nearly trod on him, they did not find him. It began to rain, the drops became heavier and heavier until there was a real downpour. When the

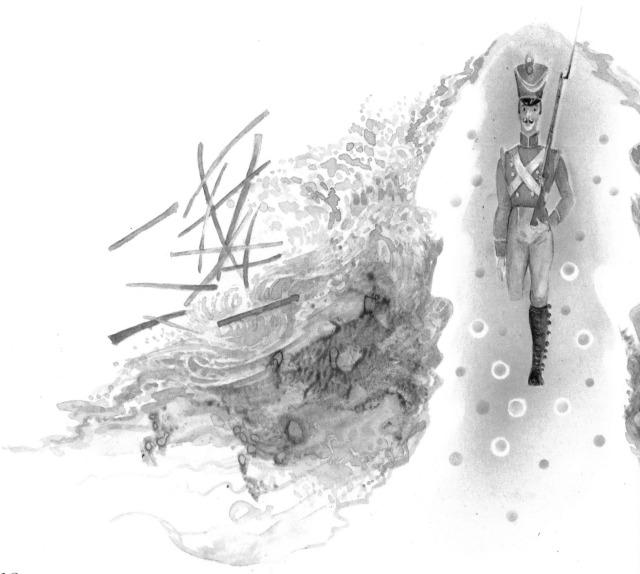

rain stopped, two boys came running along.

"Look!" one exclaimed, "there's a tin soldier! He can go sailing."

Then they made a boat out of newspaper, put the tin soldier in it and set him sailing along the gutter. The two boys ran along beside him, clapping their hands in delight. What big waves there were in the gutter and what a strong current! The paper boat rocked from side to side. The soldier put on a brave face, just looking straight ahead and keeping a firm grasp on his musket.

All at once the boat disappeared under a wide bridge.

"Where am I going?" he thought. "Ah, if only the doll was in the boat I wouldn't care if it was twice as dark!"

Just then a large water-rat that lived in the drain darted out.

"Have you got a passport?" asked the rat.

"The soldier said nothing.

"Show me!"

But the tin soldier kept silent and grasped his weapon still tighter. The boat sailed on and the rat ran after it. Ugh! how it gnashed its teeth and called out,

"Stop him! Stop him! He hasn't paid customs duties! He hasn't shown his passport!"

The stream was growing stronger and stronger. The tin soldier could now see daylight at the end of the tunnel, but he could hear a roaring sound, which was so loud it frightened even a brave soldier. Where the tunnel ended, the water from the gutter plunged down into a wide canal. That was as dangerous for the tin soldier as it would be for humans if we fell down a huge waterfall.

He was already so near that he could not stop. The boat rushed on and the poor tin soldier stood as upright as he could. No one could accuse him of being afraid. He was so brave that he did not even move an eyelid. The boat whirled round three or four times and filled up with water. It must sink. The tin soldier stood up to his neck in water as the boat sank lower and lower. The paper was becoming soggier and soggier. The water closed over the little soldier's head. He thought of the pretty dancer who he would never see again and these words rang in his ears:

"Be brave, be brave, little soldier,
For death is awaiting you!"

At that moment the paper tore and the soldier fell out. But he was swallowed up at once by a big fish. Oh, how dark it was in there! It was even worse than in the tunnel and what's more, it was very cramped, too. The little soldier was very brave and lay still, clasping his musket in his hand.

The fish swam on until it suddenly began lashing about. Then it lay quite still. Suddenly light broke in and a voice cried out, "The tin soldier!" The fish had been caught, taken to the market, sold and brought home to the kitchen where the cook had cut it open with a knife. She seized the soldier and brought him into

14

the living room. Everyone wanted to see the remarkable tin soldier who had travelled in the fish's stomach. To his amazement, they stood him up on the table and he saw the very same children and the same familiar toys on the table, including the splendid castle with the beautiful little dancer. She was still balancing on one leg. The tin soldier was so moved that he almost wept tin tears but that would not have been proper for a soldier. He gazed at the dancer and she gazed back, but they said nothing to each other.

Suddenly one of the little boys picked him up and threw him into the stove. No one knew why the boy did this but no doubt the goblin in the snuff-box had something to do with it.

The tin soldier stood in a blaze of light, overcome by the heat. He did not know if it was caused by the fire or the love that burned within him for the dancer. He had lost all colour. He gazed at the little doll, she gazed at him and he felt himself melting, but he continued to stand bravely with his musket resting on his shoulder.

At that moment the door opened and the draught caught the little dancer. She flew like a fairy, straight to the tin soldier and into the fire. She flared up and was gone. The tin soldier had melted. The next day when the servant girl took the ashes out of the grate, instead of the soldier she found a little tin heart. All that remained of the dancer was her brooch, and that was burnt as black as coal.

The two sisters and the wizard

There were once two sisters who were as beautiful as the sun and moon. One morning before daybreak Mary, the elder of the two, went out into the meadow to wash her face in the morning dew so that she would look even prettier. But she didn't return home and no one knew what had happened to her.

In vain her parents looked for her and her younger sister grieved for her. She was just nowhere to be found.

Betty told her parents that she would set out to look for Mary. She must find her sister even if she had to search the whole world for her.

At first her parents did not like the idea. They were afraid they would lose this daughter, too. But eventually they gave in. Betty's father gave her a gold coin to take with her so that she would not starve on the journey. Her mother gave her a little bag with a reel of thread, a needle, a few pins, a thimble and a pair of scissors, so that she would not have to travel about the world in torn clothes.

Betty said farewell to her parents and left. She walked on and on, travelling many days and nights, asking everyone she met whether they knew anything about her sister. No one had seen Mary and no one had heard anything about her. Then one old man said that there was a place with a stone hill, on top of which a wizard had built a castle. The wizard used spells to torment the people who lived around him. He might well have Betty's sister in his power.

The girl lost no time and made straight for the stone hill. She did not have to look for long, it towered above everything else as a high, smooth rock. There were no trees, no bushes, not even a blade of grass growing on the hill. As soon as Betty set foot on it, she slipped backwards.

She was wondering what to do, when a rattling sound suddenly came to her ears. She looked round and saw a young man struggling with a cart piled high with pots and pans. The front wheels had got stuck in a crack between some stones and he could not pull it out.

"Would you be so kind as to push the cart so that I can continue on my way?" he asked.

"Why, of course I'll help you," said Betty and leant with all her weight against the cart. She pushed hard and, all of a sudden, the wheel jumped out of the crack.

19

"You have to work hard," Betty panted. "Haven't you got a horse or a donkey to pull your cart?"

"No, I haven't. I'm the poorest wretch in the world," sighed the young man and started to leave.

Then Betty took out of her bag the gold coin her father had given her, and said,

"Take this gold coin and buy a donkey with it, so that you won't have to suffer like this any more."

The young man took the gold coin, looked gratefully at Betty and said,

"I have passed by this stone hill many a time and I have asked many people for help, but you are the only one who has taken pity on me. In return, I will tell you something that I have never told anyone before. If you want to get to the top of the stone hill, you must take your shoes off. The only way of getting to the wizard's castle is barefoot. And once you are there, don't believe what you see and hear."

Betty thanked the young man for his advice, took off her shoes and began to climb the stone hill. She did not slip backwards.

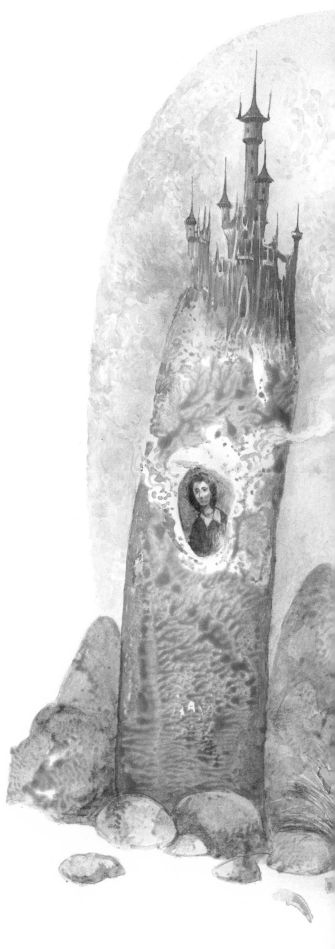

Half way up the hill she noticed another young man sitting on a flat rock. His clothes were torn and he was pinning patches on them with thorns. The thorns kept breaking and he had to pin the patches over and over again.

"You are wasting your time, young man," said Betty. She took the pins that her mother had given her out of her bag. She gave them to him so that he could pin his patches with them. The young man was glad and looked gratefully at Betty, exclaiming,

"I've been sitting here for a long time, pinning on my patches. A few people have passed by, but not one of them – except you – has taken pity on me. In return I'll tell you something I haven't told anyone before: if you keep your wits about you, you'll achieve your goal."

Betty thanked the young man for his advice and continued climbing up the stone hill. Soon she was standing before the wizard's castle and she knocked boldly on the big iron door.

The wizard opened it and asked,

"What has brought you here, young lady?"

"I've come for my sister, Mary. Give her to me. I won't go home without her."

"Come in," grunted the wizard under his breath, "but I won't give her to you just like that, for nothing."

He led her into a room and said,

"Wait for me here. I'll be back soon."

Betty sat down on the stool and waited. All of a sudden a cloud of smoke blew out of the hearth and fierce flames sprung in her direction. The girl became frightened and wanted to run out of the room. Then she remembered what the young man to whom she had given the gold coin, had said: "Don't believe what you see and hear in the wizard's castle." She calmed down and remained seated on the stool.

"Whatever will be, will be," she thought, comforting herself. At this, the smoke disappeared from the room and the flames withdrew back into the hearth.

The fire flickered quietly, as before.

Then a pitiful voice broke the silence.

"Betty my dear sister, come here, let me embrace you!"

She was just about to get up and follow the voice when she once more remembered what the young man had said. She therefore remained motionless on the stool and to make sure that she would not go running towards the voice, she tied herself to the stool with the thread her mother had put in her bag. She wound it round and round herself until she had used it all up. Then the voice stopped calling her.

When silence had fallen again, Betty cut through the thread with her scissors and got up from the stool. At that moment the door opened and the wizard entered the room. He was frowning and grunted,

"Come with me you clever little miss. I'll take you to your sister. If you recognize her, you can take her home."

23

They passed into the next room. It, too, was empty, except for seven statues standing in the middle. They were all as white as snow and looked as if they had been cast in the same mould.

"Well, which is your sister?" the wizard grinned. "If you find her, I'll let you both leave my castle. But if you don't find her, I'll change you into a statue, too!"

Betty walked in front of these statues, but she could not tell which could be her sister. The wizard began to get impatient.

24

"Take a better look, clever boots!"

Then Betty remembered the advice of the young man to whom she had given the pins: "If you keep your wits about you, you'll achieve your goal!".

She quickly put her hand into her bag, pulled out the thimble and tried it on the first statue, whispering,

"Thimble, dear thimble, help me find my sister, Mary!"

The thimble slipped off the statue's finger and fell to the ground.

"That's not my sister," Betty thought. The thimble fell off the fingers of all the other statues, except the last one. Here it stayed on the middle finger and shone like a little sun.

"That's my sister, Mary!" Betty exclaimed and threw herself round the statue's neck. The statue came to life, its cheeks grew pink, its hair turned shining gold and its blue eyes shone with happiness.

The two sisters caught each other by the hand and hurried out of the castle together.

The wizard flew into a rage. He summoned a fiery wolf to chase them. But Betty knew what to do. She pulled the needle out of the bag, threw it at the wolf's paws and cried out,

"Needle, needle, save us!"

At this the needle began dancing here and there, chasing the wolf until it plunged over the edge of the chasm.

The wizard was even more enraged. He stretched out his black cape and flew after the sisters in the guise of a bat. But Betty kept her wits about her. She caught up the bag and began beating off the bat with it. The moment it touched the bat, the wizard disappeared into thin air.

The sisters stood for a while rooted to the spot. Then from behind them came a rumbling sound. The wizard's castle had collapsed, and all that was left was a pile of stones.

Now the two sisters could climb down the stone hill in peace. Half way down, they met a young man who smiled at them. He was dressed in fine clothes, only instead of buttons, he had shining pins. He joined the sisters and the three of them went down the hill together. No sooner had they reached the bottom, than they saw a coach standing in the road. There was a young man waiting there, who Betty recognized as the one she had given the gold coin to.

He smiled and called to them,

"Take your seats in the coach. I'll drive you home."

How the old couple rejoiced at the sight of their daughters! They welcomed the young men as their daughters' future husbands and made preparations for the wedding. From then on they all lived happily ever after.

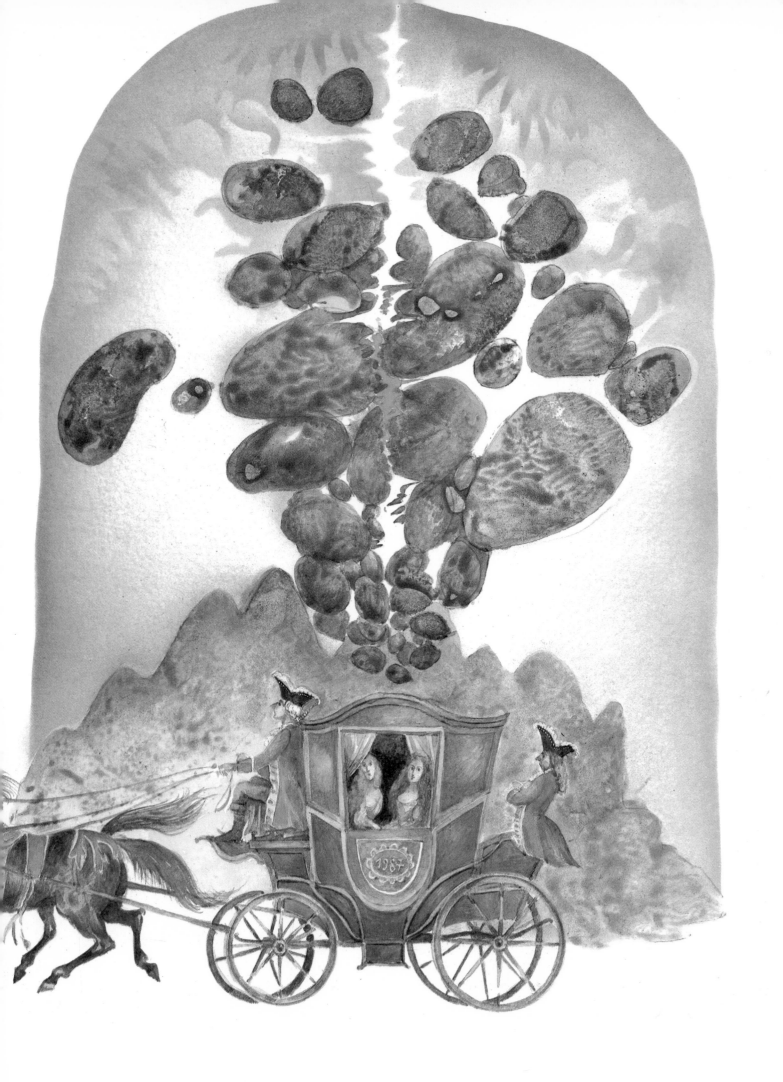

How the mice
aired their gold coins

A long, long time ago in a mountain village there lived two brothers, Taro and Naro. From morning until night they worked in their tiny field, but still did not manage to keep hunger and poverty away from the little house in which they lived.

One morning in the autumn they woke up to an unusually beautiful day. The sky was clear right from early morning, not a cloud in sight and streaked with gold from the rays of the sun.

"We can't stay at home on such a beautiful day," said Taro to Naro. "Let's go into the forest and get some wood ready for winter."

And so they went. They turned off the road along a path, walking deep into the forest until they were wandering among the trees. The green grass was fresh with dew, the scent of pine trees hung in the air and birds flew over their heads. At last they came to a rock.

"Let's rest for a while. We'll have enough wood by the time evening comes," said Naro.

They sat down and gazed into the distance. The forest rustled behind them and the sea sparkled far below.

As the brothers sat there, they suddenly heard the sound of little voices singing;

> *"We've too much gold underground*
> *We'll bring it up to air.*
> *Spread it out on the dark green moss,*
> *The sun will make it glitter there."*

The brothers looked at each other in wonder.

"Who can that be singing?" Naro asked his brother.

They looked under the rock and to their amazement they saw some mice crawling out of a crack. They were pulling bags of

28

gold coins behind them, which they emptied out on the green moss.

The brothers just stared and stared, they could not believe their eyes. The sun poured down its golden rays, and the coins suddenly shone blue, red, violet, silver and gold.

"Take them, Taro, take them, Naro!" the wind whispered in their ears as it flew by. "The mice won't notice if a few coins are missing!"

"We mustn't even touch the gold coins, they're not ours!" Taro replied.

"Don't be silly!" the wind whistled. "Take them while you still have the chance!"

"No! No one has offered them to us and we've done nothing to

deserve them! We haven't helped the mice in any way!"

"You are stupid, stupid!" howled the wind, "you are throwing away your chance of being rich!"

Taro refused to listen to the wind any longer; he picked up his axe and urged his brother,

"Come on, Naro, we've already had a rest. Come on, we must prepare some wood for the winter!"

"Wait a moment," Naro mumbled. "I'm going to take just a couple of gold coins from that pile!"

Naro filled his bag with gold coins and strode after Taro. They chopped wood all day long and it was only when the sun began to go down that they set out for home.

When they approached the white rock, they heard the mice singing again,

"Our gold now glitters like the sun,
But darkness is a-falling.
Gather it up and carry it down,
To bed, night is a-calling."

By the time they reached the rock, the mice had carried away all the gold coins. Some on their backs, some in their paws and the remainder was put in bags and pulled after them through the crack in the rock. Not one gold coin was left on the ground.

"It's a good thing I didn't listen to you, brother," Naro said to Taro. "The mice won't miss the gold coins I have in my pocket and they'll help us out of our poverty."

They set off at a pace down the hill and were soon home again. They threw their bags on the bench and stared in surprise. Taro's fell with a heavy thud and Naro's as light as a feather.

Taro looked into his bag and there he found a pile of shining gold coins. Naro opened his bag and found nothing but dry leaves.

In vain they went back to the rock. The mice never aired their money again.

How the animals turned the bear over

It was winter in the forest and everything was frozen, everything was covered with snow. Not a day passed without a snowstorm. The animals and birds were suffering from starvation, only Brum the bear knew nothing of all this. He was sleeping in his den, stretched out on his side and was not in the least inclined to turn over. That was unfortunate, because as all the animals in the forest knew, only when the bear turned over on to his other side, would the sun roll out of its winter bed and drive the cold away.

So one morning the animals decided to wake the bear up. They came to his den and called out,

> *"Wake up, wake up, don't sleep so long,*
> *New Year has come and gone.*
> *All have suffered, some have died,*
> *Turn over on your other side."*

But the bear did not hear the animals. He was sleeping a deep, deep sleep and didn't even twitch a hair. In vain did they call out,

"Wake up, wake up! Call for the sun, call for the spring! Turn over on to your other side! You've lain on this one long enough!"

Brum the bear stirred, opened one eye and mumbled,

"I won't turn over. I don't feel like it."

"I'll peck you with my beak, you lazy thing!" the crow cawed, but the deer hushed him.

"Wait a minute, you must be careful how you speak to the bear. You might offend him."

"Dear Brum, dear bear, please turn over on your other side and call for the sun. We are cold and hungry."

But the bear only grunted,

"I'm not cold, I'm not hungry. Why should I chase the winter away?"

33

At this a blue tit chirped up,

"You should be ashamed of yourself, Brum. All you think of is your own good. The trees, bushes and the seeds on them are all hidden under the snow. We've nothing to eat. Please turn over onto your other side."

"No, I won't. I don't feel like it!" grunted the bear. "What do I care about seeds, bushes and trees. Do as I do, and wait until spring comes."

"The animals looked sadly at each other and began to wander off in all directions. At that moment a mouse stuck its head out of the snow and squeaked,

"You don't mean to say you are afraid of Brum the bear? Why do you waste so much time persuading him? He's lazy. You have to talk to him in our way. If you like, I'll have a word with him. I'll make him turn over on to his other side whether he wants to or not!"

"What can a little mouse do to such a giant?" the animals exclaimed.

"Do you want spring to come, or don't you?" squeaked the mouse.

"Of course we do," said the animals. "But how are you going to turn him over?"

"Like this!" said the mouse. She ran into the bear's den and

began to tickle him. She scampered over his head, down his back, tickling his paws and nose and squeaking,

"Turn over onto your other side! Turn over and chase the winter out of the forest!"

The bear jerked his head, rolled over on to his back, his paws waving in the air and giggled,

"Stop that, mousy, enough, enough! I'll turn over, I'll turn over, just please stop tickling me!"

Brum turned over on to his other side and at that moment the sun jumped out of his bed into the sky. The clouds opened and began to warm the earth. Every day spring drew nearer. How the forest rang with joy!

Who will find the sun?

Far, far away there lies a very thick forest. Many, many animals and birds live there.

When the birds were waking the animals one morning, something extraordinary happened. The sun, that golden ball, appeared in the sky as usual but then suddenly disappeared. The sky blackened and darkness fell on the earth. The animals were frightened and began wailing,

"Where has the sun gone? How are we to find food if we can't see anything?"

At that moment an owl flew out of an old tree trunk and hooted,

"The lizards have stolen the sun from the sky. I saw them grab it and run away with it."

"What are they? Who are they?" exclaimed the birds.

"Lizards live beyond three rivers, beyond three hills, between three rocks," hooted the owl. They hardly ever come out of their underground kingdom because they don't like daylight or sunshine. One of you must go there and take the sun from them.

While the animals were pondering this, the squirrel spoke up,

"Let the bear go. He is the biggest and strongest of all the animals in the forest. He is not afraid of anyone."

"We'll send the bear to get the sun!" the animals cried out. But the owl rolled its big, round eyes and said,

"We must consider the matter carefully. The bear is big in size and he has strength enough. But don't forget that he has a sweet tooth. What if he should happen to come across a nest of bees on the way? He'll begin feasting on the honey and he'll forget all about us and our suffering. The bear would not bring us the sun, that's for sure."

The animals and birds looked sad but they soon had another idea.

"Let's send the wolf. Next to the bear, the wolf is the strongest animal in the forest. We are all afraid of him. He would surely manage to force the lizards to tell him where they have hidden the sun and bring it back to us.

"We'll send the wolf! We'll send the wolf!" the birds chanted.

But the owl rolled its eyes once again and hooted,

"Don't forget that the wolf is very greedy and unreliable. If he happens to come across a rabbit or a deer on the way, he'll run after his prey and forget all about us and our suffering. The wolf wouldn't bring us the sun either."

The birds and animals were clearly getting desperate.

"Who, then, will find the sun for us? Who will bring it and set it back in the sky?"

At this a mouse piped up.

"We'll send Bunny Long-legs. He's neither big nor strong, but there isn't a better runner in the forest. He'll be at the lizards' hideout in no time; he'll snatch up the sun and bring it back here. Then somehow or other we'll get it back into the sky.

The animals looked at each other in surprise.

"Bunny? But he's afraid of everything! He'd never find the sun! If there's so much as a rustling in the leaves, he'll forget all about us and our sufferings!"

The owl rolled its eyes.
"Let him go. He's timid, it's true, but he's reliable." The animals began to urge the little rabbit:

"Run, Bunny, run,
Fly like the wind!
Run, Bunny, run,
Bring us back the sun!"
The rabbit sat up on his hind

legs, puffed out his chest, pricked up his ears, twitched his nose and wondered in which direction to run. Should he save his skin or look for the sun. After a moment's hesitation he shot off and ran and ran and ran . . . Not once did he stop, not once did he look round.

He jumped over one stream, jumped over another and a third. He ran uphill, downhill and before he realized it, he was among some rocks. He sat up on his hind legs, pricked up his ears, twitched his nose and opened his eyes wide in wonder. For there, under one of those rocks, a blaze of light could be seen.

The rabbit shaded his eyes with his paws and peeped through the wooden door. Sure enough! Under the rock was a cave and in it was hidden the sun.

Bunny Long-legs leant all his weight against the door until it

flew open. He caught hold of the sun, heaved it up onto his shoulders and began running back so fast that the wind whistled past his ears.

It took but a moment for the lizards to come to their senses. They ran out of their underground hideout and cried,

> *"Stop, Bunny, stop,*
> *Bring us back the sun,*
> *Stop, Bunny, stop*
> *What is it you have done?"*

But the rabbit had no intention of stopping. On he ran, as fast as the wind. He darted round bushes, jumped over tree stumps. But the sun was enormous and it weighed heavily on his shoulders. The lizards were catching up and shouting after him,

"Stop, Bunny, stop,
Give us back the sun.
We'll catch you, we'll beat you
For all that you have done."
"I won't give it back!" shouted Bunny. "The sun belongs in the sky, not in a cave." He banged the sun with his fist and, to his surprise, it broke into two pieces. He threw the smaller piece upwards; it did not fall back to earth but flew up into the sky and shone there as the moon.

42

The lizards stopped in their tracks, and stretched out their paws in an effort to reach the moon. But it was too high for them. While they were discussing what they should do, Bunny Long-legs ran way ahead.

They suddenly realized what was happening and they ran after him, gaining ground all the time. Their feet thudded, eyes bulged, tongues hung out. They very nearly caught Bunny, but all of a sudden he threw the other half of the sun into the air. No sooner had he done this, than the sun shone in the sky and everything around radiated with a golden glow. The lizards hissed and fled as fast as their legs would carry them to their underground hideout. Never again did they show their faces.

The man, the buffalo and the tiger

Once long, long ago there was a jungle where all kinds of strange trees full of enticing fruit grew. Many exotic flowers grew in the jungle, too.

The inhabitants of the jungle — a striped tiger, elephants, screeching monkeys, brightly-coloured parrots and butterflies with golden wings — had everything they could wish for. They ate whenever they wanted to and whatever they felt like eating. They spent the time sleeping or playing. When they were too hot they drank at the clear spring, and when they were hungry they had food within reach of their paws, beaks or trunks.

The elephants were particularly fond of bananas, which they could easily reach with their trunks. The parrots preferred all kinds of berries and seeds, and the monkeys chose coconuts, dates and oranges. The butterflies needed no more than the refreshing nectar from the sweet-smelling flowers. The striped tiger, who considered himself to be the lord of the jungle, chose his food from that which the others offered him. In this way they lived in comfort and harmony for a long time.

One hot afternoon, when the striped tiger, monkeys, elephants, parrots and butterflies were resting in the shade of the wide branches of the trees, a black buffalo appeared in the jungle. He was not alone. A young man was sitting on his back.

The tiger raised his head, rolled his eyes angrily and growled,

"What are you doing here in the jungle, black buffalo? You have become the servant of man. What do you want?"

"It is as you say, noble lord of the jungle," said the black buffalo. "I serve man. I am better off with him. I have come to beg you to give us a piece of land where my master could grow food for himself and for me."

The elephants, monkeys and parrots, who had heard everything, laughed out loud and the striped tiger growled once more.

"Have you forgotten, black buffalo, that all the riches of the jungle, the fruit, trees, every foot of ground, belongs to me and that I have never given anyone even the smallest piece of it? However, so that you won't say I have a heart of stone, I'll give you a strip of swampy ground at the very edge of the jungle. Do you agree?"

The black buffalo shook his head unhappily, because he thought that the ground which the tiger was offering him was infertile. But the young man who was sitting on his back whispered something in his ear. Then the black buffalo said to the striped tiger,

"I agree, powerful lord of the jungle. I can see that you are noble and therefore I believe that you will keep your word. My master and I will take that swampy strip at the edge of the jungle and we will force it to give us a rich harvest. But promise in turn that you will never ask for it back."

"You are huge in size, black buffalo, but you have a tiny brain. Haven't I given my word? And anyway, what would I, powerful lord of the jungle, do with such swampy wasteground?"

The black buffalo said no more, he just gave the tiger a deep bow and went with the young man to the nearby village.

From this time on, every day, as soon as the sun had appeared over the horizon of the sea, through the afternoon heat, they worked on the piece of ground that the tiger had given them. They tore up the bushes, carried off the rocks, ploughed the land with a wooden plough and when there was not a blade of grass left on it, the young man sowed rice in the deep watery furrows.

"You're wasting your time and strength, black buffalo," growled the tiger from time to time as he passed by. "Neither you nor your master can conquer the jungle. Your fields will be swallowed up as soon as it begins to rain!"

But the black buffalo and the young man took no notice of his words. They worked hard in the field, more and more often looking up at the sky. They were waiting for the rains to come.

At last the sky clouded over. Rain began to fall from the heavy black clouds. It rained the whole day, the whole week, the whole month. The field at the edge of the jungle turned green. Heavy ears of rice appeared there.

Now the elephants, monkeys and parrots often came to the edge of the jungle to look at the wonderful sight.

"Why is it that we big, strong animals must go hungry?" they asked each other. They were indeed hungry because the rains

had beaten down the ripe fruit from the trees, the flowers had withered and the coconuts had fallen into the grass. The monkeys were too lazy to look for them there. They asked the striped tiger to take the field away from the black buffalo and the young man. The tiger kept his word and so the monkeys, elephants and parrots had to steal up to the rice field from time to time and grab at a few tasty ears of rice. They do it to this very day.

The black buffalo has remained faithful to man, helping him in his work. In return, man gives him enough food so that he need never be hungry.

The shaggy goat
and the hedgehog

There was an old goat
That hid its shaggy coat
Among the hills and rocks,
In the den of a fox.

Once a shaggy goat ran away from the village and hid in a fox's den under a dead fir tree, and stayed there.

The fox came home to find a strange animal in its den. It rolled its eyes and shrieked,

"What kind of an animal are you? Get out of my den!"

But the goat had no intention of obeying the fox. It got up, stamped its hoofs, butted out its horns and blasted,

"I am an old goat
With a shaggy coat.
I'll kick you and bite you,
Beware my horns when I fight you!"

The fox took fright and ran away through the forest, howling in terror so that the leaves shook on the trees and the pine needles fell from the branches. It met a wolf who asked,

"Why are you howling, sister fox? Why are you running so fast through the forest?"

"Oh, brother wolf, who wouldn't howl?" the fox said, wringing its paws. "There is a strange animal in my den. It stamps its hoofs, butts out its horns, it won't let me into my house, it doesn't want to leave my den! What shall I do now?"

"Don't worry. Come with me. I'll chase him out!" said the wolf.

Together they went back to the den and the wolf cried out,

"What kind of an animal are you in the fox's den? Come out at once!"

49

But the goat had no intention of obeying the wolf. It stamped its hoofs, stuck out its horns and bleated,

"I am an old goat
With a shaggy coat.
I'll kick you and bite you,
Beware my horns when I fight you!"

The wolf took fright, too. Now they both ran howling through the forest and the leaves shook on the trees and the pine needles fell from the branches.

A bear stuck his head out from a raspberry patch.

"What are you two howling about? Why are you running through the forest so fast?"

"Oh, dear bear!" the fox said, wringing its paws. "There is a strange animal in my den. It stamps its hoofs, butts out its horns, it won't let me into my house and it won't leave my den! What shall I do now?"

"Don't worry. Come with me. I'll chase him out!" said the bear.

"I tried to chase him out, but he didn't go!" wailed the fox. "And brother wolf tried to chase him out, but he didn't go. And you won't get him out of my den either!"

"Just follow me. I'm the strongest and biggest animal in the forest. I'm not afraid of anyone! Don't tell me I can't chase that beast out of your hole!"

All three of them returned to the den together and the bear roared in a powerful voice,

"What kind of animal are you in the fox's den? Come out of there at once!"

But the goat had no intention of obeying the bear. It stamped its hoofs, butted out its horns and bleated,

"I am an old goat
With a shaggy coat.
I'll kick you and bite you,
Beware my horns when I fight you!"

Even the big, powerful bear took fright. He took to his heels and tore aware as fast as his legs could carry him. The fox and the wolf fled after him. So, now there were three of them running through the forest howling and roaring until the leaves on the trees shook and the pine needles fell from the branches.

A hedgehog poked its head out of the undergrowth.

"What are you three howling about? Why are you running through the forest so fast?"

"Oh, dear hedgehog," said the fox, wringing its paws. "There is a strange animal in my den. It stamps its hoofs, butts out its horns, it won't let me into my house and it won't leave my den. What shall I do now?"

"Don't worry. Come with me. I'll chase him out!" said the hedgehog.

"You?" wailed the fox again. "I tried to chase him out and he didn't go, brother wolf tried to chase him out and he didn't go. Not even the big, powerful bear could chase him out. How on earth do you think you, a tiny hedgehog, will get him out?!"

The bear and the wolf also muttered impatiently.

"Us lords of the forest have already been there and tried, but we didn't succeed in chasing him out. You won't get him out either!"

"You may be kings and lords of the forest, while I am just a tiny hedgehog, but I will chase this animal out of the fox's den!"

He curled himself up into a ball and rolled down the hill, the fox, wolf and bear ran at breakneck speed after him.

When he came to the fox's den the hedgehog uncurled himself and called out,

"What kind of an animal are you in the fox's hole?" Come out at once!"

But the goat had no intention of obeying the hedgehog. It stamped its hoofs, butted out its horns and bleated,

"I am an old goat
With a shaggy coat.
I'll kick you and bite you,
Beware my horns when I fight you!"

But the tiny little hedgehog did not take fright.

"And I am a hedgehog
With a prickly coat.
You think I'm no match
For a shaggy old goat?"

He curled up into a ball and rolled into the fox's den. He rolled around all over the place, pricking the goat in its tenderest spots where the shaggy fleece had fallen off. The goat bleated and shrieked in agony, ran out of the den and tore down the hill as fast as his legs would carry him.

The fox thanked the wolf, the bear and the hedgehog for their help, trotted into its den, curled up and fell asleep. The bear and the wolf slipped off into the forest. And what about the tiny little hedgehog? He crept back into the undergrowth, where a comfortable bed of soft leaves awaited him. He lay down and started nibbling at the pile of crab apples he had collected in the autumn.

Why dogs show their teeth

There once lived a man who had two beloved animals, a dog and a cat. The dog was old, without a single tooth, but he knew all the roads in town. The cat was still young and she was afraid to go far from her master's house because she knew neither the roads nor the pavements in town.

One day the man said to his beloved animals,

"You will take this ring to my daughter in the next town. I will give it to you, Pussy, because you are very careful. And you, Doggy, show the cat the way and don't allow anyone to take the ring from her."

The cat and the dog promised to do as their master told them, and set out. They came to a river but there was no bridge in sight. The dog and the cat tried to find a boat, but in vain. However, they didn't give up. In those days cats liked swimming, just as dogs and people do, although they couldn't swim very well.

The dog was afraid that something would happen to the ring. He said to the cat,

"Give me the ring while we swim across to the other bank. I'm afraid you will lose it."

"No, no," said the cat. "Our master entrusted me with the ring, so I will keep it."

"You'd better give it to me," urged the dog. "It'll be safer with me while we cross the river."

"No, I won't give it to you! I won't, I won't!" the cat spat back at him.

The dog got angry and began to bark fiercely,

"Will you give it to me, or won't you?" and he approached the cat threateningly, intending to take the ring by force.

The cat was afraid and gave him the ring. "If you lose the ring it won't by my fault," she whined.

They stepped into the water and began swimming. The current was so strong that they were soon worn out. The cat was being dragged downstream and she was just wondering whether to return to the bank when she heard,

"I've lost the ring! The water has carried it away!"

The dog was very unhappy.

"You see, I told you!" the cat reproached him. "Let's go home and tell our master."

"No, I'm going to look for the ring," said the dog and he began diving under the surface of the water.

Although he tried very, very hard, he did not find the ring. In the end the dog and the cat set out for home.

On the way, the dog was overcome by fear and he fled into the woods.

"I didn't expect you back so soon," said the man, when the cat

arrived home. "Did you give the ring to my daughter?"

The cat shook her head.

"Where is the dog?" asked the man, realizing that the cat was alone.

"He ran off into the woods, sir, because he lost the ring!" the cat said, and then burst into tears.

"The dog lost the ring?" shouted the man. "Didn't I tell you not to give the ring to anyone?"

The cat told him exactly what had happened. The man flew into a rage and cried,

"I must punish that dog!"

He summoned all the dogs in the town and ordered them to hunt down the culprit.

"If you bring him back here I'll reward you with gold," he said. No one knows why he promised them gold instead of bones. Gold doesn't interest dogs in the least but all dogs love bones. He promised them gold and it seemed as if that was just what they all wanted.

56

"How can we tell him from other dogs, sir?" they asked.

"He hasn't a tooth in his head," said the man. "Bring him back and I'll shorten his tail as a punishment."

And so the dogs set out to look for the culprit. They hunted here, there and everywhere, but there was no trace of the dog.

Since that day, dogs have been looking for the dog that lost the ring. Whenever a dog meets another one it asks,

"Are you the dog that lost his master's ring?"

And they all give the same answer to this question,

"No!" and they wag their tails and show their teeth. "Look! I've got all my teeth!" they say to each other. "The dog that lost the ring hadn't a tooth in his head."

And so they go on searching for him to this very day.

The cat learned her lesson from this experience and has never swum again.

How the rabbit
bought his boots

Bunny Longears had two gold coins and he set off to the fair with them. He wanted to buy some warm boots for the winter.

He was hopping down the forest path when suddenly a fox jumped out of the bushes. The fox was dressed up in a warm fur coat and on his feet he had just the kind of boots that the rabbit wanted to buy. They greeted each other and continued down the path together, because the fox was on his way to the fair too.

As they trotted along, the rabbit could not keep his eyes off the boots, he liked them so much. Finally he asked,

"How much did you pay for those boots, brother fox?"

"Two gold coins."

The rabbit was glad to hear that and exclaimed,

"I have two gold coins. I'll buy some boots just like that!"

The fox pretended that he had not heard about the gold coins, but he began to make plans how to get them from the rabbit.

Very soon the sky grew dark and it began to rain. That wouldn't have mattered so much, but evening was approaching and the wet rabbit began to feel cold. He was shivering all over, but he put on a brave face and trotted on.

Suddenly the fox said,

"Listen, brother rabbit, we shall have to stay the night somewhere or we'll catch cold."

"Where can we stay the night when we don't know anyone for far and wide and we have no money to pay for a bed?" lamented the rabbit.

"You needn't worry about that," the fox assured him. "There's an inn under that old pine tree. It's kept by a bear. He'll put us up for the night and then in the morning we can continue on our way."

"Don't forget, brother fox, that you have to pay for a bed," the rabbit said stubbornly, "and I've only got two gold coins for the boots I want to buy. You stay at the bear's inn, I'll curl up somewhere under a fir tree."

"Nonsense," grumbled the fox. "Who wants your two gold coins? You just come with me and I'll get you a bed and some supper, too, I'm not as poor as you are!"

The rabbit let himself be persuaded and went into the inn with the fox. The bear welcomed them, sat them by the fire and while they warmed themselves he disappeared into the kitchen to prepare the supper.

The rabbit sat in front of the fire and shook all over. Not from cold now, but from fear. After all, who had ever heard of a rabbit, a fox and a bear spending the night together under the same roof?

"Will roast meat be to your liking?" the bear called from the kitchen.

"Yes, that will be fine, just hurry up and put it on the table," called out the fox. However, the rabbit protested in a high voice,

"I'm not hungry. I won't have any supper. And I haven't any money with me to pay for it anyway."

"Be quiet! Didn't I say I'd take care of the bill?" said the fox angrily. "You just tuck in to whatever the bear gives us."

No sooner had he said this than the bear came in wearing a white apron and a chef's hat. He placed a tray on the table with meat, honey cakes and a jug of milk. Then he sat down at the table with them to watch them enjoying their supper.

The fox grabbed the meat and when he had gobbled it up, he started on the honey cakes. Before the rabbit realized what was happening, the jug was empty and there wasn't a crumb left on the table.

"You've eaten your fill, so now pay for your supper," said the bear. "Then I'll show you where you can sleep."

"How much do you charge for the supper?" asked the fox.

"Seeing it's you, two gold coins."

The fox began turning out the pockets of his fur coat, but there was no money to be found there. So he turned to the rabbit.

"Pay for the supper, brother rabbit, I've left my purse at home. I'll borrow the two gold coins from someone at the fair and I'll give them back to you there."

The rabbit wailed,

"I told you we shouldn't come here! You know very well I've only got two gold coins with me and I need those to buy boots!"

"Pay up or . . . !" growled the bear.

"Let the rabbit pay, he dragged me in here!" barked the fox.

"That's not true," squeaked the rabbit. "It was the fox who persuaded me to stay here for the night. He ordered the supper, let him pay for it!"

"Pay up, you rascals, or you'll regret it!" roared the bear and caught hold of a heavy stick he had hidden behind the door.

What could the rabbit do? Weeping bitterly he pulled out from his pocket a scarf in which he had screwed up the gold coins and he gave them to the bear. The fox drank the milk which was left in the bottom of the jug, stretched himself out on a bench and fell asleep. Then the bear also took himself off to bed and the rabbit was left at the table by himself.

Bunny Longears sat at the table and pondered over his misfortune, when his eyes suddenly fell on the boots which the fox had taken off. He did not think twice, he put them on and hopped off home.

In vain the fox looked for him at the fair and in the woods. The rabbit took great care never to meet him again. He kept well away from him, even though he knew that he had bought the boots. Whether at the fair in town or from the fox, it was all the same. He had paid for them honestly with his own gold coins.

The deer
and the jaguar

One day a deer was wandering along the bank of a river and muttering to himself.

"I've had a hard life. I've wandered here and there and I've never had a house of my own. I'd like to have one at last. Where could I find a better place than this? I'll build it here. And he trotted off.

The very same day a jaguar thought,

"My life is all care and suffering. I'll find a place, build a house and live in it."

He looked and looked until he came to the place where the deer had stood a short while before. Here he halted and exclaimed,

"Where could I find a better place than this? I'll live here!" And he ran off.

Next day the deer came back and began to build a house. It was hard work. He had to clear away the bushes and trees and level the ground. When he had done this, he left, intending to return as soon as he could.

The next day the jaguar arrived, planning to begin building his house and what should he see – the ground had already been cleared and levelled. "Oh!" he said. "The Spirit of the Forest is helping me! What good luck!"

So he continued with the work. He laid the floor and when it was dark, he left.

In the morning the deer returned. The floor was ready! He said,

"Oh! The Spirit of the Forest is helping me build my house! What good luck!"

He built the walls and went back into the forest. Next day the

jaguar came and saw that the walls had been built.

"Thank you, Spirit of the Forest!" he called out and made the roof. Then he disappeared into the forest. When the deer returned he found the roof ready. He said,

"Thank you, Spirit of the Forest, for your help!"

Out of gratitude he made two rooms in the house, one for the Spirit of the Forest, the other for himself. Then he went into his room and lay down to sleep.

That night the jaguar appeared again. He went into the empty room to sleep and he thought he was living together with the Spirit of the Forest who had helped him to build his house.

64

In the morning the deer and the jaguar got up at the same time. The jaguar asked in surprise,

"Was it you who helped me to build this house?"

The deer said, "Yes, it was. And was it you who helped me to build this house?"

The jaguar said, "Yes, it was. Well, if we have built this house together, we'd better share it."

The deer agreed and they lived together, one in one room and the other in the other.

One day the jaguar said, "I'm going hunting. I'll bring something to eat and you prepare the cooking pot, water and wood for the fire."

He went off into the forest and the deer meanwhile prepared everything necessary for cooking.

The jaguar killed a deer in the forest and brought it back to the house. When the deer saw what kind of an animal he was living with, he was very unhappy. The jaguar cooked his prey, but the deer refused to eat it.

The jaguar ate his fill and they both went to bed. The deer thought in horror about the jaguar's supper and could not sleep. He was afraid the jaguar would come in the night to kill him too.

In the morning he said to the jaguar,

"You get the pots ready and prepare the water and wood. I'm going out hunting."

He went off into the forest, where he caught sight of a powerful jaguar sharpening its claws on the bark of a tree. The deer trotted on until it found an anteater. He said to him,

"That jaguar said all kinds of bad things about you."

When the anteater heard this, he flew into a rage. He stole up behind the jaguar and killed him. Then he left.

The deer dragged the lifeless jaguar back home. The pots, water and wood were already prepared. But when the jaguar saw what the deer had brought, his appetite deserted him.

That night neither the deer nor the jaguar could sleep. The jaguar was afraid that the deer would come and kill him, and the

deer was terrified at the thought that the jaguar would attack him in the middle of the night.

As the night went on, they both lay quietly, wide awake. But towards morning they were overcome by drowsiness. The deer's eyes closed and his head sank. At that moment his horns hit the wall with a loud thump.

The jaguar heard the noise and started up in fright, thinking that the deer was coming for him. He roared out in terror.

The deer heard the jaguar roar and was convinced that he was coming for him. Both animals dashed out of the house into the forest. The deer in one direction, the jaguar in the other. They never returned to the house again and from that day to this they have not lived together.

Father and Mother of the forest

There once lived a young man who liked hunting. One day he decided to get a rabbit for his supper. He slung his gun over his shoulder and set out into the forest. He wandered here and there, but could not see a rabbit anywhere. He was just about to return home when he almost fell over a family of young wood grouse. He quickly took aim, but then hesitated.

"It would be a pity to kill them. They're so small, they can only

have hatched a short time ago. Let them enjoy life and run around in the forest."

He turned away and went on. Soon he came to a little lake in the forest, where he almost tripped over a frightened wild duck. It had a broken wing and could not fly away, so it just scrambled through the grass as best as it could. The young man could have caught it with his bare hands if he had wanted to, but he hesitated,

"It's probably got a family of ducklings in its nest to look after. Let it live, perhaps its wing will heal soon."

He left the duck in peace and went on his way. Suddenly he heard branches breaking and a stag ran out of the undergrowth onto the forest path. It was as big as a horse, with horns like the branches of a tree. The young man was just about to cock his gun and take aim when he was struck by a thought.

"Can I kill something so beautiful? Let him wander through the forest and lead his wives and children to graze."

He wanted to go on his way, but then he saw that the path had suddenly disappeared from under his feet and he was

70

surrounded by thick undergrowth. In the middle of this stood a little house. The doors and windows were open wide.

"Who on earth can live in this thicket?" the young man wondered, and peeped in through the window. He saw a room with a large wooden table in the middle, at which there sat an old man with a long, mossy beard. An old woman was sitting at a distance from him and spinning.

"Good evening," the young man said to them. The old man lifted his head and said,

"The same to you, young man. Welcome and come in. Take a seat and have supper with us while you're here."

No sooner had the young man sat down at the table than it was covered with all kinds of food. Plates made of birch bark had appeared, laden with gifts of the forest: hazel nuts, crab apples, strawberries, raspberries and bilberries. In the middle stood a birch wood jug full to the brim with a liquid of some kind.

"Help yourself," the old woman urged the young man. "When you have eaten your fill and drunk of the birch sap in the jug, you can lie down over there and in the morning continue on your way. You must stay here for the night."

"Who are you, good folks? You are not magicians of some kind, are you?" the young man asked.

"We are who we are. We look after the forest, so that all is as it should be there. We show ourselves only to those who deserve it."

"And what have I done to deserve your kind hospitality?" the young man was even more surprised.

"You have done plenty. You did not kill the young wood grouse that almost tripped you up, you took pity on the wild duck with the broken wing and even the sight of the stag did not make you greedy. So how could we turn you away from our house? Eat your fill and rest for the night."

As soon as dawn broke the next day the old man said,

"Get up, young man. You must set out on your journey if you want to arrive home before dusk. I'll take you to the path that leads to your home."

He put a birch hat on his head, birch bark shoes on his feet and

over his shoulders he flung a cape of birth leaves. The old woman gave the young man a box of birch wood and said,

"Take this as a souvenir. May that which is inside remind you of us."

The young man thanked them for the supper and the present and for putting him up for the night and followed the old man down the mossy path. They went on and on. It was almost evening when they came to a clearing in the forest.

"You must go on from here by yourself. You don't need me any more," said the old man. Before the young man could thank him he had vanished in the haze of the forest.

When the young man arrived home, he put the box of birch wood on the table and told his father and mother what had happened.

"They were good people, they fed me and gave me a bed for the night, only they did not tell me who they were."

"That can have been no other than the Father and Mother of the Forest!" exclaimed his parents. They opened the birch wood box and took out the three seeds that lay in it. They planted them beside the fence and placed the box next to the well.

By the time evening came, the box had grown into a graceful birch tree and the seeds had sprung up into three beautiful trees: a red mountain ash, a proud fir and a fragrant pine.

The straw bullock

There once lived a Grannie and a Grandpa. They were very poor indeed. One day Grannie said to Grandpa,

"Make a bullock out of straw and cover it with tar!"

"What use would a straw bullock be to us, Grannie?" Grandpa asked in surprise.

"You just make it, I'll find a use for it!"

Grandpa made a bullock from straw and covered it with tar. In the morning Grannie took some hemp, drove the straw bullock out to graze and said,

"Graze, bullock, graze in the middle of the meadow, until I have spun my hemp into rope."

She sat down in the grass and began spinning. She spun and spun, until she began to doze.

At this moment a bear ran out of the black forest and muttered,

"Who are you?"

"I am a bullock, not three days old, made of straw and dipped in tar!"

And the bear said,

"If you are tarred, give me some tar, let me mend my fur coat with it. Look what a hole the forester's dogs have made in it."

"Help yourself!"

The bear caught hold of the straw bullock, meaning to take some tar with his paw. But he stuck to it and couldn't free himself. In vain he pulled and pushed, twisted and turned. He had no choice but to drag the bullock off with him into the forest.

Grannie woke up to find the bullock was no longer in the meadow. She looked around and caught sight of the bear dragging the bullock into the forest, unable to free himself.

She lost no time and ran for Grandpa,

"Grandpa, Grandpa, the straw bullock has caught a bear!"

Grandpa hurried off into the forest, brought the bear home and shut him up in the cellar.

The next day Grannie took the bullock to graze once more. She drove it out into the pasture and said,

"Graze, bullock, graze in the middle of the meadow, until I have spun my hemp into rope!"

She sat down in the grass and began spinning. She spun and spun, until she began to doze. At this moment a wolf ran out of the forest and growled at the bullock,

"Who are you?"

"I am a bullock, but three days old, made of straw and dipped in tar."

"If you are tarred, give me some tar. Let me mend my fur coat with it. Yesterday it was torn by the forester's dogs!"

"Help yourself."

The wolf bit into the bullock, meaning to take some tar, but his teeth got stuck. Try as he might, he could not pull them out of the tar. He twisted and turned, but could not free himself from the bullock. He had no choice but to drag it off with him into the forest.

Grannie woke up and saw the wolf making off into the forest with the bullock. She ran for Grandpa, shouting,

"Grandpa, Grandpa, our bullock has caught a wolf!"

Grandpa hurried off into the forest, brought the wolf home and shut him up in the cellar with the bear.

On the third day she again drove the bullock out to graze. She sat down in the grass, began to spin and said,

"Graze, bullock, graze in the middle of the meadow, until I have spun my hemp into rope."

She spun and spun until she began to doze. At that moment a fox ran out of the forest.

"Who are you?" she asked the bullock.

"I am a bullock, but three days old, made of straw and dipped in tar."

"Then give me a little tar," the fox begged. "The forester's dogs have torn my fur coat and it needs mending."

"Help yourself."

The fox bit into the bullock, but her teeth got stuck in the tar. As she twisted and turned and threw herself about, she woke up Grannie, who at once ran to fetch Grandpa.

"Grandpa, Grandpa, our bullock has caught a fox."

Grandpa brought the fox home, too, and shut it up in the

cellar. The he sat down in front of the door and began to sharpen his knife.

"Grandpa, Grandpa, why are you sharpening your knife?" called the bear from the cellar.

"I'm going to take your fur coat. I'll make it into two fur jackets, one for Grannie, one for myself."

"Let me keep my fur coat, Grandpa, you'd do better to set me free. I'll bring you honey!"

"Then bring me honey," said Grandpa. He let the bear out of the cellar and went on sharpening his knife.

"Grandpa, Grandpa, why are you sharpening your knife?" asked the wolf.

"I'm going to take your fur coat, I'll make two warm hats for winter from it. One for Grannie and one for myself."

"Let me keep my coat, Grandpa, you'd do better to free me. I'll bring you a flock of sheep."

"Bring me some sheep," said Grandpa. He let the wolf out of the cellar and went on sharpening his knife. The fox pricked up her ears and asked,

"Grandpa, Grandpa, why are you sharpening your knife?"

"I'm going to take your fur coat and make two warm collars for winter from it. One for Grannie and one for myself."

"Oh, don't take my coat from me, Grandpa, let me go free. I'll bring you some hens."

"Bring me some hens," said Grandpa and let the fox out of the cellar, too.

Early next morning, even before the sun had appeared over the horizon, there came a banging on the door. Bang, bang, bang! Grannie woke up and said,

"Grandpa, Grandpa, someone is trying to get in. Have a look and see who it could be!"

Grandpa went out and what should he see — the bear had brought him a whole bee-hive of honey.

A short while after there was again a banging on the door: bang, bang, bang!

The wolf had driven a whole flock of sheep into the courtyard. A minute later the fox appeared with geese and hens.

Grannie and Grandpa were delighted. They sold the sheep and bought a live bullock. Grandpa used it to carry wood from the forest. They had no need for the straw one. They left it in the courtyard and forgot all about it, so it melted in the sun.

The bear
and the mosquito

A bear once caught a rabbit in the forest and began, just for the fun of it, to pull its ears. The rabbit cried out in pain and humiliation. But the bear was enjoying himself, he just went on pulling and laughing, twisting the rabbit's ears first in one direction, then in the other.

When the bear had amused himself to his satisfaction, he let the rabbit go and went on his way.

The rabbit crept into hiding under a bush, crouching there half dead from fright, wiping its tears with its paws and lamenting,

"What a wretched creature I am, small and weak, with no one to defend me."

"I'll defend you," the rabbit suddenly heard a whistling sound in the bushes.

He looked round and caught sight of a mosquito. He cheered up so quickly that his eyes were dry in a flash.

"How can you, a little insect, be a match for a bear?"

"I'm stronger than the bear," said the mosquito. "I can torment him and make him cry. I won't let him sleep. Tomorrow you'll see for yourself."

It was very hot and the bear didn't know where to hide himself from the stifling heat. In the end he lay down in the shade of a thick tree. No sooner had he shut his eyes than he heard just above his ear.

"Bzzz, bzzz . . ."

"Curse it," grumbled the bear and waited for the mosquito to settle on his nose.

The mosquito circled over the bear and then landed on his nose. The bear lost no time and gave his nose a smack. But the

mosquito was not stupid, he flew off before the bear could strike him.

No sooner had the bear turned over on his other side, than he heard once more,

"Bzzz, bzzz . . ."

But after a while the buzzing stopped. The bear thought that the mosquito had flown away. But the mosquito had no intention of leaving the bear in peace. He quietly crept into his ear and bit him there. The bear howled in pain, rolling to and fro he banged his paw on his ear so hard that he saw stars jumping before his eyes. Then he rubbed his ear and made himself as comfortable as possible, so that he could get some sleep at last. But there was no hope of that! No sooner had he closed his eyes than the sound of

the mosquito's buzzing came from above his head.

"That silly mosquito! He just won't give me any peace!" grunted the bear. He got to his feet and lumbered off to find another place for the night.

The bear pushed its way through the bushes, scratching himself, yawning loudly and with the mosquito at his heels,

"Bzzz, bzzz, bzzz . . ."

The bear broke into a run. He ran and ran and at last, completely worn out, he stretched himself out under a tree. He lay and listened: silence reigned in the forest, only the rustling of the leaves was to be heard. All the animals and birds had fallen asleep long ago. It was dark, nothing to be seen. He shut his eyes and at that moment from just above his ear came,

"Bzzz, bzzz, bzzz . . ."

The bear sat up and burst into tears,

"So you're not going to give me any peace, you good-for-nothing? I'll get you, even if I have to sit here until daybreak!"

But the bear did not kill the mosquito, even though he almost tormented the bear to death.

In the morning the sun rose. The birds and animals woke up. They joyfully welcomed the new day; only the bear was not glad to see the sun. He wandered here and there through the woods, bad-tempered and sticky from the heat, his eyes drooping from exhaustion and his ears still ringing from the buzzing of the mosquito.

The rabbit saw the bear and almost jumped for joy.

"Who would have thought the mosquito could be such a fine fellow?"

He hopped around and giggled until the tears ran down his cheeks.

The mosquito heard him and came flying up to him. He asked, "Did you see the bear?"

"Yes, I did, I did," said the rabbit and giggled so hard he had to hold his stomach. Thank you, you're a good friend. But tell me, how did you – such a little creature – manage to get the better of such a large bear?"

"That's simple," said the mosquito. "We mosquitos are not such timid things as you rabbits."

The girl
called Mona

There was once a little girl who didn't like walking. Because she was always moaning, people called her Mona.

Mona had a good-tempered, white-haired Grandmother. Once they went off to the meadow to pick flowers. When they had gathered a bunch of white ox-eye daisies and blue bell-flowers, they set out for home. Mona soon became tired of walking. She stopped in the middle of the path and whined,

"Pick me up! My legs ache!"

Grandmother laughed and said,

"Don't be silly. Big girls like you can walk. I can't pick you up or carry you on my back."

They went on for a while, but then Mona again stopped and began complaining,

"Who will carry me home? Grandmother won't wait for me . . ."

Bunny Longears came running up and squeaked,

"I'll carry you!"

Mona sat on the rabbit's back and off he went down the path. But rabbits are timid creatures and when this one heard something at the roadside, he ran off to hide in the woods. He crouched down beside a tree trunk and lay there as if frozen to the spot. Only his whiskers twitched nervously. Mona didn't wait for Bunny Longears to recover from his fright. She climbed onto a tree stump and cried out,

"Who will carry me home?
Grandma won't wait,
Bunny fears his fate . . ."

A snail was sliding past the tree stump. It looked up at Mona and whispered,

"Get on my house, I'll take you home!"

Mona got onto the snail's house and the snail set off. The sun shone down on them and before she realized what was happening, Mona fell asleep. When she woke up about half an hour later, she saw that the snail had not even covered the distance from one tree stump to the next. She jumped down from his back and cried,

"Who will carry me home?
Grandma won't wait,
Bunny fears his fate,
The snail takes all day . . ."

Mona caught sight of a billy-goat grazing in the meadow. It bleated,

"Meee, meee. Get up on my back. I'll carry you home!"

Mona sat astride the goat's back and the goat set off. First it threw up its hind legs, then its front legs and before Mona could shout, "Be careful, I'll fall off," she was on the ground.

She got up, dusted herself down and turned to tell the goat what she thought of it, but there was no sign of it anywhere. And so she called out,

"Who will carry me home?
Grandma won't wait,
Bunny fears his fate,

88

The snail takes all day,
The goat's run away . . ."
A grasshopper came hopping
up to Mona and chirped,
"I'll carry you home. Sit on me!"
It stretched out its feelers and
waited for the girl to climb onto
its back. Mona caught hold of its
feelers, but as soon as the
grasshopper leapt into the air,
she slipped off into the grass.

Mona lay in the grass and
moaned,

"Who will carry me home?
Grandma won't wait,
Bunny fears his fate,
The snail takes all day,
The goat's run away.
The grasshopper tries to fly . . ."

A dove appeared above her head and cooed,

"Coo coo, coo coo, I'll carry you! Hold tight to my wings!"

Mona held tight to the dove's wings and the bird soared into the sky. It flew so high that she felt quite giddy.

"Dove, dear dove, put me down!" she screamed. "I'm

afraid I'll fall!"

Beneath them a stream stretched out like a thin blue ribbon. The dove circled over the water and landed on the bank. It took a drink of water, flapped its wings and flew off. Mona found herself alone again. As she looked round she saw that a little boat was floating on the water. She wiped her tear-filled eyes and called out,

"Who will carry me home?
Grandma won't wait,
Bunny fears his fate,
The snail takes all day,
The goat's run away.
The grasshopper tries to fly,
The dove soars too high . . ."

The boat bobbed on the waves and rustled,

"Sit down in me, I'll carry you . . ."

Mona sat down in the boat and floated along. But the boat was made of paper and very soon it began to fill with water. Fortunately, the bank was near. No sooner had Mona jumped out of the boat, than it sank.

Mona stood on the bank of the stream and wailed,

"Who will carry me home?
Grandma won't wait,
Bunny fears his fate,
The snail takes all day,

91

The goat's run away.
The grasshopper tries to fly,
The dove soars too high,
The boat's disappeared . . ."

A bee was flying along the bank and it buzzed,

"Bzzz, Mona. Stop moaning. Your own legs can carry you home. Follow me, I'll show you the way!"

At first Mona just dragged herself along, but then she began to walk at a brisker pace and before she realized it, she was home once more.

The fisherman and
the golden duck

Long, long ago in a cottage at the edge of a lake there lived a fisherman named Martin and his young wife. Martin was a cheerful, hardworking fisherman. He never pulled his net out of the water empty. His wife was the best spinner and weaver for far and wide. No one could weave more beautiful linen and tablecloths than she.

One day, however, the young woman and her loom

94

disappeared. No one knew where she had gone. People were surprised and talked about it for a long time, but eventually they forgot her. Only Martin could not stop thinking about his wife.

Once, when he was sitting at the lakeside fishing, he caught sight of a hawk circling above him. It hovered for a long time in the blue sky before diving headlong into the reeds growing at the edge of the lake. When it rose in the air again, it was clutching in its claws a golden duck. Martin picked up a stone in anger and flung it at the hawk. The hawk immediately let go of the golden duck and flew off.

The golden duck then limped up to the fisherman and quacked,

"I know what's on your mind. You helped me when I was in trouble, so now I'll help you."

"I won't ask anything of you," the fisherman sighed, "but just tell me, if you know, where my wife disappeared to, she was the best spinner and weaver in the country around."

"Your wife is now in the palace of the Lake King," quacked the golden duck. "The water nymphs carried her off to weave them transparent gowns and veils."

"Water nymphs in the lake?" Martin exclaimed in surprise. "I've never seen them and I've never heard anything about the Lake King and his palace."

"Do as I tell you and all will be well," quacked the golden duck. "Pull a feather out of my right wing. Before the sun rises throw it into the thickest patch of mist hanging over the lake. Then sit quietly on the bank and wait to see what happens . . ."

The golden duck flapped her wings and as soon as Martin had plucked the shining golden feather, she disappeared into the reeds.

In the morning, by the time the first rays of light appeared, Martin was already at the lake. He could hardly see it because it was shrouded in white mist. He wasted no time, threw the golden feather into the thickest patch, and wonder of wonders! The mist over the lake vanished, revealing water nymphs singing and dancing.

"Catch one of them and don't let her go!" quacked the golden duck from the reeds. Martin nodded and the moment the water nymphs danced nearer to the bank, he caught the youngest of them by the hand.

"Let me go, the sun will rise any moment now," the nymph begged. "I mustn't let its rays fall on me."

"I'll let you go, but first take me to my wife, the best spinner and weaver for far and wide!" declared fisherman Martin.

Just at that moment the tip of the sun appeared over the horizon. The nymph wrapped her transparent veil around Martin and sank into the lake with him.

"Where have you been so long, little daughter? And who have you brought with you?" the Lake King called to her from his water palace.

96

"I am Martin, a fisherman, and I have come for my wife, the best-known spinner and weaver in the region. Give her back to me, Lake King. I won't return home without her."

The King of the Lakes looked at Martin and said,
"You have courage, fisherman. But don't imagine I'll let our spinner and weaver go just like that. You can take her from my palace only if you fulfil three tasks. This is the first. In the garden next to my palace there grows a tree, the like of which is to be found nowhere in the world. It used to have pink and white flowers every year. But recently it has been fading and withering. If you save it and it flowers again, you will have fulfilled the first

task. And now my youngest daughter will take you back to the bank and in the morning, as soon as dawn begins to break, you will tell me how to save the tree."

Grave and sad, Martin sat down at the edge of the lake and pondered over the difficult task. At that moment the golden duck came swimming up and quacked,

"I know what's worrying you, fisherman Martin. You are afraid that you will not be able to make the lake tree flower and that you wife will never see the sunshine again. Isn't that it?"

Fisherman Martin nodded.

"Don't worry. Tomorrow morning tell the Lake King that his favourite tree will revive and flower again if he digs up the anchor which is rusting under its roots.

No sooner had the Lake King's servants dug up the anchor than the tree turned green and began to grow.

"Now I'll give you your second task, fisherman," said the delighted Lake King. "I need three golden feathers from the golden duck which nests in the reeds at the edge of the lake."

Martin brought him the golden feathers and declared boldly,

"Tell me the third task, Lake King!"

"Look closely at the gowns and veils that my daughters wear. They glitter with the silver light of the stars. It was woven into them by your wife. If you can tell me who will decorate the gowns of my daughters, the water nymphs, instead of your wife, you can take her home."

Martin could not have fulfilled this task if it had not been for the golden duck. As soon as he emerged from the lake, she swam out of the reeds and quacked,

"No one can help you now, fisherman Martin, except the Queen of the Night. Beg her for help when she appears, to reign over the lake!"

Martin sat down at the edge of the lake and as soon as it was dusk and the birds settled down in their nests for the night, the Queen of the Night stretched her dark velvet cloak over the lake. A crown of stars twinkled on her head and the moon glittered on her forehead.

Martin bowed before the Queen of the Night and told her of his suffering. When he had finished, the Queen of the Night stretched out her dark velvet cloak even wider, bent over the lake and called,

"Let the spinner and weaver go, Lake King. From now on I, the Queen of the Night, shall weave the shimmering light of the stars into the veils and gowns of your daughters!"

What joy there was when the young woman emerged from the lake! The Queen of the Night adorned the grass and trees around with her silver light. And in the morning, as soon as the mist had cleared from the lake, on its surface the flowers of the lake tree blossomed in all their beauty – the pink and white flowers of the water lily.

The thirteen flies

There once lived a weaver who didn't like to work. He preferred to spend the whole day sitting on a bench in his garden, or walking along the river bank with his hands in his pockets. And, so, whatever had to be done in or around the house had to be done by his wife.

Nobody ever saw him sitting at the weaving loom, even though he always had beautiful, fine woollen cloth to offer whenever a buyer appeared.

Nobody ever saw him in the garden with a spade either. It was his wife who bent over the rows of vegetables from spring to autumn so the harvest was good. Her flowers and fruit caught the eye of every passer-by.

When, from time to time, the woman's eyes came to rest on her lazy husband, she just could not understand how he could be so idle. It gave her no peace and she lay awake night after night. The weaver, however, would go to bed as soon as the sun set, happily snore through the night and wake up in the morning well rested.

Once, when the woman was tending the vegetables in the garden, a swallow flew over her head.

"Don't worry, good woman! I'll help you out of your troubles! Just send your husband to the fair tomorrow!"

"How can you help me, dear swallow, when he takes no notice of what I say?" the woman shook her head sadly.

"Don't worry, just do as I say. Send him to the fair and you'll see."

The next day, as soon as dawn broke, the woman woke her husband and sent him to the fair to sell cloth.

The weaver set out in a good mood. As he went along, the sun began to shine brighter and brighter and sweat began to pour down his face. Then the swallow flew up and circled round his head.

"Don't be in such a hurry," she whispered to him. "You've got a good part of the journey behind you, have a rest for a while."

The weaver was surprised, but even so he decided he would sit down under a tree and have a little rest. He put down the hamper of cloth next to him, pulled his hat down over his eyes and very soon he fell asleep. When he woke up, the same swallow was flying around him and she dropped a nut as big as a hen's egg at his feet.

The weaver was again surprised. He picked up the nut and turned it over and over, looking at it from all sides. He even put it to his ear, because it seemed to him that he could hear a rustling sound coming from it.

"What's this meant to be?" he wondered. He put the nut into his pocket and went on his way.

He couldn't get the nut out of his mind and kept taking it out of his pocket and putting it back again. When he put it to his ear

again, he heard not a rustling but a buzzing sound. It was not long before he could make out the words,

> *"If you value your life,*
> *Open the nut with your knife!"*

The surprised weaver opened the nut. In a flash out flew thirteen flies, the size of bees. They buzzed around his head,

"If you don't give us work, we'll bite you till it hurts!"

The weaver saw that it was no joke and he racked his brains,

"Carry me to the market!"

Before he realized what was happening, he was at the market. But the flies kept on buzzing around his head,

"If you don't give us work, we'll bite you till it hurts!"

He sold the cloth and hurried home with the flies after him. They kept buzzing around him even more angrily,

"If you don't give us work, we'll bite you till it hurts!"

His wife threw her hands up in fright when he ran into the courtyard.

"For heaven's sake, give them something to do or they'll torment me to death!" screamed the weaver.

"Churn the butter, drive the goat from the meadow, bring in the cloth which is bleaching on the grass," the woman shouted.

104

In a minute everything was done. But the flies swarmed around again and this time not only around the man's head, but around the woman's, too.

"If you don't give us work, we'll bite you till it hurts!"

In vain they chased them with the broom, they swiped at them with the duster, but the flies would not go away. All the orders the flies were given were carried out to the last word and in a flash. And as soon as everything was done, they buzzed back to the weaver and his wife with threats that they would bite them.

The weaver and his wife could not think of anything else for the flies to do.

Then the weaver's wife called out,

"Swallow, dear swallow, help us, or this plague will ruin us!"

The swallow flew up with a whole flock of birds. In no time they had eaten the flies, and enjoyed the feast.

The weaver and his wife sighed with relief, thanked the swallow for her kind help and set to work. They washed the windows and doors and aired the whole house.

Since that day, whenever the weaver felt like taking a rest while he was at work, it was enough for him to hear the buzzing of a fly, and his laziness vanished at once.

Bearskin and her seven brothers

In an Indian settlement there once lived seven brothers. They had one sister whose name was Bearskin. She was extraordinarily strong and could carry a thick tree trunk on her back as if it were a bundle of sticks. She walked with a heavy, clumsy step. Wherever she trod, the grass withered and the ground was left bare. She wasn't even afraid of wild animals. Coyotes and foxes were her friends but her favourite was a huge grizzly bear, which lived in a dark cave in the forest. Bearskin used to take him ripe strawberries and sweet honeycombs. And when she stroked his shaggy back, she wished very much that she was a she-bear and not a human. But in the tops of the trees she used to hear the leaves whisper:

"Wait, Bearskin, wait, your time will come one day!"

When she told her brothers at home that she often went to the rocky cave, they were afraid for

106

her, because the grizzly bear was very fierce and dangerous. The whole of the Indian settlement was afraid of it. Only Onikar, the youngest brother, was proud of his brave sister and felt a respect for her as for a powerful being.

Bearskin lived in this way until it was time for her to get married. Then her eldest brother said,

"Dear sister, we should be very happy if you took Beavertooth for your husband. He is a brave Indian hunter that lives on the other side of the great lake."

Bearskin shook her head,

"I can't take Beavertooth for my husband, brother, because he is not strong enough."

Then other young men came who wanted her as a wife, but she gave them all the same answer. Very soon people began saying that she was obstinate and fussy, until the whole settlement frowned on her. Only Onikar still loved his sister and was devoted to her.

Once when the older brothers went off hunting, Bearskin said,

"Onikar, I don't want to live in the settlement any longer,

because everyone keeps talking about me. I shall leave you and go to live in the rocky cave with the grizzly bear. He understands me better than people do. I wish you well."

With these words she left home and set off into the forest.

When people in the settlement heard this, they said,

"A girl from our tribe cannot live in a rocky cave with a bear. We must kill it. Then Bearskin will return to the settlement and will marry one of the warriors, as is the custom in our tribe."

They gathered together, took their arrows, spears and tomahawks and set out into the forest. They crept up to the cave, threw themselves at the sleeping bear and killed it before it could even wake up.

The girl threw her arms around him, weeping bitterly and took from his chest a piece of the bear's fur to remember him by. She hid it in the bag under her belt. And at that moment a strange thing happened. Bearskin began to lose her human appearance, until she had completely changed into a huge she-bear.

The people from the village took to their heels in terror and

the she-bear chased after them with a terrifying growling. Who knows what would have happened, if her youngest brother, Onikar, had not stood in her way. When she saw the look of anxiety on his face, she took control of herself, calmed down and once again turned into a human. She begged him to let her live in his house and he agreed, even though he was afraid of her.

In the evening the other six brothers came home, too. When they heard what had happened, they said,

"We can't have her here, she'd be a constant threat to us."
But Onikar reminded them,
"Don't forget, she *is* our sister."
In spite of this, the brothers chased Bearskin away into the mountains. All through the night they collected thorns and thistles and scattered them around the little house in which she slept. Then they slept, too.

Bearskin ran out of the house; when she saw what her brothers had done, she flew into a rage and changed into a huge bear.

The brothers did not wait, they ran off as fast as their legs would carry them, but she ran after them.

"Onikar, save us!" they shouted, terrified.

They could already hear the grunting of the she-bear when Onikar blew around him and cried,

"May bilberries grow behind me for as far as my breath can reach."

In a flash a patch of bilberries appeared behind the brothers. Bearskin could not resist them. While she was tasting them, the brothers covered a good distance, but when the she-bear had eaten her fill, she ran after them and was soon at their heels again. Then Onikar shot an arrow in the air and cried,

"May there tower behind me rocks as high as my arrow flies!"

Steep rocks appeared across Bearskin's path. She climbed up them skilfully, but clambered down the other side with great difficulty. Meanwhile the brothers had run on. When the she-bear had managed to get down the rocks she lumbered after them. There was nowhere they could hide from her, nowhere they could escape and they thought there was no way they could

save themselves now. Then Onikar stamped his foot and cried,

"May a high tree grow in front of my brothers!"

At once there appeared a tall green maple tree. The brothers scrambled up into it and hid in the branches. The furious she-bear dug her sharp claws into the trunk of the maple and climbed up after them. The brothers did not know what to do and called out to Onikar,

"Onikar, take aim at her with your bow, or she will kill us all."

But Onikar replied,

"It's our sister, I can't kill her."

He looked around him, desperately wondering how to save his brothers. But he could think of nothing. Finally he looked up at the sky. It was full of shining stars, only just above his head there was an empty space. Now he knew what to do. He took some arrows out of his sheath, and one by one shot them straight upwards over his head. With every arrow he shot, he cried,

"Brother, fly up to the stars!"

When he had shot six arrows, he himself sat on the last one and flew after them. The she-bear calmed down and, grunting to herself, set out for the rocky cave. Her seven brothers still live in the sky as stars and together are known as the Great Bear.

The singing frog

Once upon a time there lived an old man and woman. Every day the old man would go to work in the vineyard and at noon the old woman would take him his lunch.

One day the old woman sighed, "How nice it would be to have a granddaughter, even if she was as small as a frog. She would help me in the house and brighten up our lives."

She had hardly finished speaking, when a little green frog appeared at her feet. It rolled its beady eyes and said,

"Here I am, Grandmother. Put the bag of food on my back. I'll take it to Grandfather while you have a rest at home."

The old woman threw up her hands in amazement. "How could you carry the bag? Why, you're a frog, you have no hands and your back is tiny."

"Just do as I tell you," said the frog.

The old woman did not like the idea, but she put the lunch bag on the frog's back and accompanied it to the door.

Hopping and jumping along the sandy path. Hopping and jumping across the green meadow. As soon as she drew near the vineyard, she called out, "Granddad, I've brought you lunch!"

The old man stopped digging the earth round the vines, looked over his shoulder and stepped back in surprise when instead of the old woman he caught sight of the bag of food, and the little green frog underneath it.

"Who are you?" he shook his head in wonder as he took the packet from the animal's back.

When she told him, the old man was glad. He sat down under a tree and began to eat his lunch happily. Meanwhile the frog leapt up onto a vine leaf and began to sing. She did not croak as frogs usually do, but sang like a fairy of the woods.

Just at that moment one of the king's sons, who was out hunting with his followers, happened to pass by the old man's vineyard. When he heard the amorous song, his heart beat fast with excitement. He halted in his tracks, listened and then called to the old man,

"Who is that singing so beautifully? I can't see anyone. If it is a young man, he shall be my brother. If it is a girl, she shall be my bride. I give my royal word of honour on it."

114

The old man was afraid to tell the prince that it had been a little green frog singing on a vine leaf. So he just said that he did not know.

The prince looked sad, but as he could no longer hear anyone singing, he went on his way.

The next day the frog brought the old man his lunch once again. While he ate, she jumped lightly on to a vine leaf and began singing. She sang far more beautifully than the day before. The old man listened to her intently.

When the frog had stopped singing, the prince appeared from behind a tree and asked, "Old man, tell me who was singing to you so beautifully while you were having your lunch?"

But the old man shook his head as if he did not know.

On the third day the prince decided that he must find out who sang so beautifully in the vineyard. While it was still early he hid behind a tree and waited. At lunchtime, when the sun climbed high in the sky, he looked down the sandy path and saw the lunch bag bobbing along. When it reached the vineyard the little frog jumped out from under it and called, "Grandfather, come and eat your lunch!"

And as soon as the old man sat down under a tree, the frog jumped up on to a vine leaf and began to sing. The prince could not believe his eyes. He crept up to the vine, picked up the frog and put it down on his palm.

"Don't be afraid, little frog," he said, "I won't hurt you. But tomorrow there is going to be a special ceremony at the king's castle, at which the king will chose his successor. He has requested his sons to bring their brides for the occasion. They are to sing him a song and present him with flowers. The bride who sings the most beautifully and gives him the most beautiful bouquet will be chosen as the next queen. I have not yet found a bride, but you could at least come to sing to the king.

"I shall come," the frog replied. "Just send a white cock to take me there."

When the prince had left, the frog hopped away to the green meadow, where she changed into a girl. She wove herself a dress out of the sun's rays, put it on and then became a frog once more.

On the next day she set out for the king's palace. A white cock carried her to the gates, but the guards did not want to let her into the courtyard. They stood in her way so that she could not pass. But the cock flew over the guards' heads and made for the courtyard.

How the prince's two older brothers and their brides laughed when they saw who was coming to meet him! But the youngest prince took no notice of their ridicule. He placed the little frog on his palm and kissed her. And no sooner had he kissed her than she turned into a beautiful girl, dressed in a golden robe. The cock did not stay a cock either. A white horse now pranced on the spot where it had stood.

Then the ceremony began. The trumpeters blew a fanfare and the king came out of the castle. He approached his eldest son's bride, Princess Haughtynose and asked her,

"What song will you sing me and what flowers will you give me?"

The princess motioned to a servant, who hurried up at once with a bouquet of rose buds. She handed this to the king and began to sing. She sang in such a shrill voice that the doves on the castle roof took flight and flew away.

The king nodded his white head and moved on to the bride of his middle son – Princess Lazybones. She just waved her hand vaguely in the direction of her servants as a sign that they should place a bouquet of sweet-smelling carnations in front of the king. Then she took to singing in a languid voice. The sparrows in the king's courtyard thought that night must be approaching and they hid their heads under their wings and fell asleep.

The king nodded his head once more and moved on to the girl in the golden robe. Before he could ask her, she presented him with a bunch of ripe wheat. Then she sang so beautifully that all those present held their breath as they listened.

When her song was over, the king smiled and said,

"I don't know who you are or where you came from, dear girl, but you have not only gladdened my heart with your song, but you have also given me the most beautiful bouquet. You and my youngest son shall inherit my kingdom.

So the singing frog became a queen. In a short time she brought the old man and old woman from the vineyard to the royal palace, and they all lived together happily ever after.

The tomcat, the cockerel and the fox

A tomcat and a cockerel once lived happily together in the forest. The tomcat would go out to chop wood and the cockerel stayed at home and looked after the house.

When the tomcat left for the forest he told the cockerel,

"Be careful, Cock-a-doodle, don't open the door, don't lean out of the window, or the fox will come and carry you off!"

The fox got to hear that the cockerel was often alone at home and wanted to catch him.

And so as soon as the tomcat had left the house, the fox crept towards the edge of the forest. She ran up to the house, sat under the windowsill and sang,

> "Oh, what a fine cockerel you are,
> There's none to compare by far,
> With your sleek black feathers and scarlet crest,
> Your yellow beak and all the rest,
> Let me sing you a song to please your ears,
> I'll make you laugh, I'll move you to tears,
> Just open your window, fling it wide,
> Such a proud cockerel should be ashamed to hide."

Cock-a-doodle was curious to know who was singing so beautifully. He opened the window and stuck his head out. The fox quickly jumped up and ran off with Cock-a-doodle in her mouth!

The fox ran on, carrying the cockerel in her sharp teeth. The cockerel screamed at the top of his voice,

> "Tomcat, dear tomcat,
> The fox has caught me,
> Is carrying me, off,
> Into the woods,

Over the glen,
To her dark den.
Scratch her with your claws,
Tear me from her jaws!"

The tomcat heard and, chasing after them, caught them up and snatched the cockerel from the fox's jaws. He brought him home and said to him,

"Don't lean out of the window, Cock-a-doodle, and don't trust the fox. The fox would eat you – bones feathers and everything."

The next day the tomcat

again set out for the woods. He told the cockerel,

"Don't listen to the fox, Cock-a-doodle, don't open the window. I'm going a long way into the forest today, I might not hear you."

No sooner had the tomcat left, than the fox ran up once more, crouched down under the windowsill and sang,

"Oh, what a fine cockerel you are,
There's none to compare by far,
With your sleek black feathers and scarlet crest
Your yellow beak and all the rest,
Let me sing you a song to please your ears,
I'll give you gold peas like shining tears,
Just open your window, fling it wide,
Such a proud cockerel should be ashamed to hide."

The cockerel walked up and down the room in silence. He didn't open the window. But the fox began singing again,

"Oh, what a proud cockerel you are,
There's none to compare by far,
With your bright black feathers and scarlet crest,
Your yellow beak and all the rest,
Let me sing a song to please your soul,
I'll give you magic seed in a golden bowl,
Just open your window, fling it wide,
Such a fine cockerel should be ashamed to hide."

This was more than the cockerel could resist. He was dying to know what magic seed in a golden bowl looked like. He opened the window just a crack and said,

"You're deceiving me, Mrs. Fox, you want to eat me!"

"Oh, dear, no, Cock-a-doodle!" the fox reassured him in a sugary voice. "Such a thing would never even occur to me. I just want you to visit me and play with my children!"

The cockerel stuck his head out of the window and – snap – the fox caught him and was dragging him away. The cockerel began screaming at the top of his voice,

"Tomcat, dear tomcat,
The fox has caught me,

Is carrying me off,
Into the woods,
Over the glen,
To her dark den.
Scratch her with your claws,
Tear me from her jaws!"

The tomcat heard the cockerel's cries coming faintly from a distance and ran in that direction. He caught up with the fox, snatched the cockerel from her jaws and brought him home.

"I told you not to listen to the fox and not to lean out of the window! Tomorrow I shall have to go even further into the forest – you'll shout and I won't hear you."

No sooner had the tomcat left the house in the morning than the fox came slinking up under the window and sang the same song,

"Oh, what a proud cockerel you are,
There's none to compare by far,
With your sleek black feathers
and scarlet crest,
Your yellow beak and all the rest,
Let me sing you a song
to delight your soul,
Magic seed shall be yours
in a golden bowl,
Just open your window,
fling it wide,
Such a fine cockerel
should be ashamed to hide."

He sang it three times, but the cockerel said nothing, the

window stayed closed. So the fox said,

"Have you turned dumb, Cock-a-doodle, why don't you answer me?"

"No, you won't trick me again, Mrs. Fox. I won't lean out of the window!"

The fox edged nearer and once more began to sing,

"Oh, what a fine cockerel you are,
There's none to compare by far,
With your bright black feathers
and scarlet crest,
Your yellow beak and all the rest,
Look out of your window, see
what I have here,
You really should trust me,
there's nothing to fear."

Then he said,

"At least show me your face, Cock-a-doodle. Don't believe the tomcat – after all, if I'd wanted to eat you, I'd have eaten you long ago! But I like you, I want to teach you all kinds of things, show you what you've never seen before. But if you don't want to, it can't be helped. I'm not going to try to persuade you any longer, I'm going home."

But she didn't go away, she just pressed up closer to the wall. The cockerel flew up onto

126

the bench, he wanted to see whether the fox had left.

He stuck his head out of the window, the fox caught hold of him and ran off with him into the dark woods, over the deep stream, up the steep hill . . .

The cockerel cried out . . . But in vain he shouted, in vain he called – the tomcat did not hear him, did not run up to save him.

The tomcat arrived home that evening to find that the cockerel had disappeared.

So he picked up his violin, slung a sack over his shoulder and set off to follow the fox's trail and free the cockerel.

He came to the fox's cottage, stopped in front of her door and began to sing and play on his violin,

"Fiddle-dee-dee, fiddle-dee-dee,
Good folks within, just listen to me,
Over hill, over dale, far and wide
must I roam,
Are Mrs. Fox and her young cubs
at home?"

The fox sent her daughter to see who was playing so well and who was singing such a beautiful song.

The daughter stepped outside and the tomcat grabbed her and thrust her into his sack. Once more he set to playing and singing,

"Fiddle-dee-dee, fiddle-dee-dee,
Good folks within, just listen to me,
Over hill, over dale, far and wide must I roam,
Are Mrs. Fox and her young cubs at home?"

The fox listened and told her son,

"Go and see who is playing and singing so beautifully!"

The fox cub stepped outside and the tomcat grabbed him and thrust him into the sack.

And then he went on singing and playing,

"Fiddle-dee-dee, fiddle-dee-dee,
Good folks within, just listen to me,
Over hill, over dale, far and wide must I roam,
Are Mrs. Fox and her young cubs at home?"

The fox listened and thought,

"I'll take a look and see for myself who is playing and singing so beautifully!"

She stepped out of the house and the tomcat grabbed her and stuffed her into the sack. Then he tied the sack up, went into the house and looked under the stove. There he found the cockerel crouching in terror. When he caught sight of the tomcat he crowed at the top of his voice with joy – "cock-a-doodle-do!"

The tomcat picked him up and took him home.

The fox and her cubs had to bite their way out of the sack. Since then, the fox has kept well away from the tomcat's home.

Ori and Princess Blue-eyes

At one time there was a kingdom ruled by King Plenty. He had a beautiful daughter, Princess Blue-eyes.

In that kingdom there also lived a young man called Ori, who since he was a child had helped his father chop wood in the forest. When he grew to be a young man, he was so well-built that far and wide there was no one who could rival him in strength and agility. He had a good heart, too, as soft as fresh bread. He never harmed the animals in the woods and he never refused help to anyone.

One day, however, a rock appeared in the middle of the king's courtyard. Nobody knew where it had come from. The king ordered his servants to remove it, but the moment they lifted it, a three-headed dragon appeared and roared,

"I'm hungry. Give me something to eat! If you don't, I'll swallow you all up!"

They threw him a calf, a sheep and a pig but the dragon's appetite was insatiable.

"I'm hungry!" he roared. "Give me something to eat, because if you don't, I'll swallow you all up!"

They threw him what they had, but when the king's storehouses and cattlesheds were almost empty, King Plenty announced,

"I shall give half my kingdom to whoever frees me of the greedy beast that has invaded my courtyard, and Princess Blue-eyes shall be his wife."

Princes of all kinds rushed to the king's court, but as soon as they set eyes on the dragon, they took to their heels and fled.

"Is there no one to be found in the whole of my kingdom who will rid me of this dragon?" King Plenty moaned.

And the dragon under the rock stuck out his heads and roared,

"Give me something to eat! If you don't, I'll swallow you all up!"

Just at that time Ori was sitting on a tree stump in the

forest and eating his lunch. A little mouse came running up to him and begged him, "Give me something to eat, young man, I'm hungry!"

He broke off a crust of bread for her and when she had eaten her fill, she said,

"Because you have fed me, I shall give you a pine needle. Take it to the royal palace. It will help you when you most need it.

Ori thought this very strange, but even so he did as the mouse had told him. When he heard the king lamenting, he declared,

"Your Majesty, I will free you of this monster!"

"You go and chop wood in the forest! You have neither sword nor princely clothes!" retorted the king.

"That doesn't matter. I'll wring the dragon's necks with my bare hands if he doesn't agree to go away of his own free will!" said Ori. He stepped up to the rock and called,

"Come out, you ugly dragon and take to your heels or you'll see what you are in for!"

As he lifted his hand the pine needle turned into a sword. Everyone stared in amazement, including the dragon, who began to beg for his life.

"Don't kill me, kind sir. I haven't hurt anyone yet. Roll the rock back and I promise that I'll never show my faces again. Lift the rock once more a year from now and you will see that I shall no longer be there!"

"Then live," said Ori and he rolled the rock back where it had been.

Everyone was glad that the dragon would trouble them no more. Only the king frowned because this was not the kind of bridegroom he had wanted for his daughter. He was sorry to have to give half his kingdom to such a poor man. However, Ori asked nothing of him, he just swung his sword over his shoulder as he would an axe and took himself off into the forest.

A few days later the king's spies brought the news that his neighbour, King Wantall was preparing to invade his kingdom. King Plenty then began lamenting once more and promised the earth to whoever would save him from disaster.

The very same day the little mouse came scampering up to Ori and when he had fed her, she gave him a hazel nut.

"Take it to the royal palace," she said. "It will help you when you most need it."

Ori obeyed the mouse this time, too, and when he heard the king's lament, he declared,

"I shall drive King Wantall and his army out of the country!"

"You go and chop wood in the forest!" King Plenty retorted. "You haven't even got princely clothes or a horse!"

"That does not matter," said Ori. He disappeared behind the rock, cracked the shell of the nut and before he knew what was happening, he found a horse with a golden mane standing beside him and his ragged clothes had changed into princely garments. He stroked the beautiful horse, leapt astride it and set off to meet the enemy. Princess Blue-eyes caught sight of him from the window and gasped,

134

"Who can that be? He looks like the young man who over-powered the dragon, and his sword is the same. But his clothes are different. If only he were to return from the battle alive and well," she sighed.

Meanwhile Ori was approaching the enemy. When the soldiers saw him slashing at the bushes and grass around him, their eyes almost popped out of their heads. They turned and

ran away as fast as their legs would carry them. King Wantall
followed suit, escaping while he still had the opportunity.

When there was no one left on the battlefield, King Plenty
emerged from his hiding place in the thick undergrowth.

"Thank you for your help, unknown prince! As a reward I
shall give you half my kingdom and Princess Blue-eyes to be your
wife."

"How can that be?" Ori exclaimed. "You have already

promised her and half your kingdom to the young man who rid your court of the dragon."

"Oh, he was only a poor wretch, dressed in rags! How could he live in my castle?"

"If that's the case, Your Majesty, let Princess Blue-eyes decide for herself who she wants to marry – poor man or prince!

As soon as Princess Blue-eyes heard this, she hurried to Ori's cottage. Ori was outside, chopping wood in his ragged clothing.

She went up to him and said,

"It's you I want to marry. You are the one who got the better of the dragon and drove the enemy out of our kingdom. Come, I'll take you to my father."

King Plenty was looking out of the window, impatiently waiting for his daughter to return. When he saw who she was bringing to the castle, he yelled,

"Don't you dare bring that wretch here! I won't give him half my kingdom nor allow you to be his wife!"

When she heard this, Princess Blue-eyes turned away and went with Ori to his cottage.

"We shall live here if father does not want us!"

The wedding took place the very same day. There were no wedding guests. No wedding feast.

When a year had passed, Ori said to the princess,

"I'm going to lift the rock in your father's courtyard. I want to know if the dragon kept his word."

When he arrived at the castle, he rolled the rock back, and before he knew what was happening he was shrouded in thick smoke, and fell motionless to the ground. That is how the princess found him when she went to look for him.

She wept as if her heart was breaking, and she did not notice the two little birds that flew over him. One was holding a green herb in its beak and the other wanted to take it. As they tugged at it the green sprig fell out of the bird's beak and landed on Ori's breast. He opened his eyes at once, took the princess by the hand and led her home.

When they arrived home, they almost fell over in astonishment. On the spot where their simple cottage had stood, there was now a beautiful palace. Behind them, instead of the king's palace there was only a rough-looking hut.

An old man in simple clothes appeared in the doorway of the hut, an axe slung over his shoulder. He stared at the rock that still stood there and then set out for the forest to chop wood.

The gingerbread man

There was once a mother who had seven children. One morning she sifted some flour, prepared the yeast, milk, butter, sugar, eggs and, not forgetting a pinch of salt, she mixed the ingredients into dough. When it had risen, she made it into a beautiful round gingerbread man and put it in the oven to bake.

The gingerbread man lay on the baking tray and grew and grew, turning crisp and brown. The seven hungry children crowded around the oven. They couldn't tear their eager eyes away from the gingerbread man.

"Mummy, give me a piece of the gingerbread man," the first child broke the silence.

"Dear Mummy, give me a bit, too," begged the second.

"Dear, good Mummy, don't forget me," cried the third.

"Dear, good, sweet Mummy, I'm hungry, too," the fourth jumped up and down in excitement.

"Dear, good, sweet, darling Mummy, cut a piece off for me, too," the fifth handed her a knife.

"Dear, good, sweet, darling, beloved Mummy, I'm here too," the sixth pressed up to her.

"Dear, good, sweet, darling, beloved, our one and only Mummy, you haven't forgotten me, have you?" asked the seventh.

"Wait a while, children, I must turn the gingerbread man over first," the mother quietened her hungry children.

The gingerbread man heard that they were going to turn him over and then eat him. He puffed himself out even more and said to himself,

"I'm not going to let them turn me over and I'm certainly not going to let them eat me! I'm going to roam through the world

and when I reach the edge I'll turn over!"

He jumped off the tray and ran off into the world. The mother ran after him with the tray in her hand, Granddad ran after her, the wisest in the land, and after him ran the seven children. A merry band, and all of them shouting,

"Stop, gingerbread man, stop! Don't run! We'll catch you and eat you anyway!"

But the gingerbread man was round and he rolled on so fast that they couldn't catch him.

At the side of the road sat a cat, Sleepy-eyed Suzie. She caught sight of the gingerbread man and miaowed,

"Gingerbread man, round as a pan, roll over here! Stop running, I'll catch you and eat you anyway!"

"You won't catch me, and you won't eat me!" cried out the gingerbread man.

"Behind me, see?
Mother, tray in hand,
Granddad, wisest in the land,
Seven children, a merry band,
They'd eat me up for tea,
But they can't catch me!"

The gingerbread man took a leap and rolled on towards the edge of the world. Suddenly a brightly feathered cock ran out of the undergrowth and crowed,

"Gingerbread man, round as a pan, roll over here. Stop

running, I'll catch you and eat you anyway!"

"You won't catch me and you won't eat me!" shouted the gingerbread man over his shoulder.

"Behind me, see?
Mother, Granddad,
Seven children and a cat —
They'd eat me up for tea,
But they can't catch me!"

The gingerbread man took a leap and rolled on towards the edge of the world. But a goose — all white and ready for a fight — crossed his path and gaggled,

"Gingerbread man, round as a pan, roll over here. Stop running, I'll catch you and eat you anyway!

"You won't catch me and you won't eat me," the gingerbread man called out.

"Behind me, see?
Mother, Granddad,
Seven children,
A cock and a cat —
They'd eat me up for tea,
But they can't catch me!"

And the gingerbread man rolled on and on towards the edge of the world. Soon he came to a puddle where a pig was wallowing in the mud. It leapt to its feet and squeaked,

"Gingerbread man, round as a pan, roll over here! Stop running, I'll catch you and eat you anyway!"

"You won't catch me and you won't eat me!" laughed the gingerbread man. He rolled around the puddle and called out,

"Behind me, see?
Mother, Granddad,

143

Seven children,
A cock and a cat,
A goose – all white
And ready for a fight,
They'd eat me up for tea,
But they can't catch me!"

The gingerbread man rolled on and on, and when he was almost at the edge of the world, he came to a wide stream. The gingerbread man rolled along the bank and he wanted to cross to the other side, but there was no way over. He couldn't jump it and he was afraid to swim across.

The pig, covered in mud from head to toe, ran up to the stream and called after him,

"Wait a minute, gingerbread man. I'll take you across the stream. Jump up on my snout and we'll be there in no time!"

The gingerbread man jumped up on the pig's snout and the pig tried to snap him up, but he couldn't. The gingerbread man jumped off and hid in the grass. The pig looked for him everywhere, snuffling through the grass and rooting in the soil, but he didn't find the gingerbread man.

It didn't occur to the pig that the gingerbread man had turned round and gone home. That is why to this very day pigs snuffle through the grass and root in the ground – they are looking for the gingerbread man, as round as a pan.

A tale
about thunder

There once lived an old man and his wife and they had an only daughter. They called her Akkanidi – Grannie's daughter.

One day in summer Akkanidi went to fetch some water. She was returning from the well, carrying two buckets full of water, when a bear appeared from behind a rock and said,

"Give me a drink of water."

Akkanidi answered, "Go and drink from the lake, there's plenty of water there."

But the bear didn't want to hear of that.

"Give me a drink of water. The water in the lake is stagnant it's no good for drinking."

So Akkanidi gave the bear a drink of water, but then he grunted,

"Now come with me to my den. If you do as you are told, you'll be well off. But if you try running away, I'll catch you!"

"And what do you want me to do at your home?"

"You will do the housekeeping and look after my reindeer."

Akkanidi turned to leave, but the bear caught hold of her, threw her over his shoulder and ran off with her into the forest as fast as he could go.

Once at home, the bear ordered Akkanidi to guard his house, feed and water his reindeer and cook lunch.

"But don't set foot in there!" He waved his paw in the direction of a hut encircled by chains.

Having said this, he went off to hunt.

Akkanidi fed the reindeer and gave them water as well. And then she set to wondering,

"Why won't the bear allow me to go near the hut?"

She got up and approached the hut until she was only a few

steps away. At that moment there came a loud rumbling roar.

Akkanidi took fright and ran away from the hut, just as the bear returned.

"Have you been in the hut?" he inquired.

"No, but I passed by it and heard a rumbling roar," said Akkanidi. "I was frightened so I ran away."

The bear went all the way around the hut, examining the chains as he went, and when he came back, he said,

"Listen to me. Don't go anywhere near that hut again. I'm going to the forest now to look for raspberries."

Akkanidi once more fed and watered the reindeer and while

doing this she happened to pass by the hut. As she was passing, she heard a thunderous voice,

"Dear girl, take these chains off me! Save me and I'll free you."

"Who are you?" asked Akkanidi. "You make such a rumbling noise."

"I am Thunder, but don't be afraid. If you free me, I'll save you from the bear."

Akkanidi took a file and began to file through the chains. She had filed half way through when dusk fell and she had to return to the hearth to cook the bear's supper.

In the morning the bear once more went off into the woods. Akkanidi hastily fed and watered the reindeer and then set to work to finish filing through the chains.

She filed right through them and out of the hut came Thunder.

"Take a sack of hay with you and a branch of fir and don't forget the tinderbox and tinder," he said.

When Akkanidi had done this, Thunder set her on his back, took a deep breath and flew so steeply into the sky that everything around rumbled and shook.

The bear heard the noise, abandoned his hunting and ran after Thunder and Akkanidi.

Thunder soared high in the air, but the bear had no difficulty in keeping up. Thunder flew – the bear leapt with great strides. When Thunder saw that the bear was catching up with them he shouted,

"Quick, Akkanidi, throw the sack of hay behind you."

Akkanidi threw the sack of hay behind her. The bear pounced

on it and tore it into little pieces. While he was clawing at it, Thunder and Akkanidi got way ahead. But it was not long before the bear was catching up again, with roars of,

"I'll catch you, I'll catch you!"

Then Thunder told Akkanidi to use the tinderbox to set the fir twig on fire and throw it into the middle of the hill of dry lichen that stretched out below them.

As soon as Akkanidi had done this, Thunder flared up in a sheet of lightning and when the bear had reached the top of the hill he was enveloped in smoke and his fur began to burn. While he was twisting and writhing in an effort to put out the fire, Thunder and Akkanidi gained ground on him once more.

The bear saw that he couldn't catch them up now, so he turned round and went back home.

Thunder took Akkanidi to the place where she had left her buckets and asked her,

"Didn't you enjoy flying through the sky? Stay with me if you want."

"No, thank you. I'm happiest with my own folk!" the girl laughed. She picked up her buckets and set out for home.

Thunder rumbled his farewell and flew back into the sky.

Since that day when the thunder rumbles in the sky some people are glad and some shake with fear.

How the wolf
went fishing

One day a wolf went to visit a distant relative of his, a fox. He found her licking her lips over a meal of fish.

"Give me a morsel of fish to taste," the wolf begged and opened his jaws.

"No, I won't," the fox replied. "Go to the river and catch as many as you want for yourself."

"I don't know how to catch fish," the wolf swallowed hard, his mouth watering.

"It's not difficult to catch fish. Bring me a jug or a bucket of some kind and I'll teach you how," said the fox.

The wolf stole a jug from a farmer in the village and brought it to the fox. As soon as it became dark they set off together for the river. The river was frozen over.

"What now? How are we going to fish?" lamented the wolf.

"Stop moaning and cut a hole in the ice," the fox advised him.

The wolf set to and as soon as he had cut a hole through to the water, the fox tied the jug to his tail and said,

"Let the jug down into the water. In the morning it will be full of fish."

The wolf lowered his tail and jug through the hole and waited. He soon shivered with cold and his teeth chattered. The fox walked round and round him, muttering something under her breath,

"Blow bitter breeze, may the wolf's tail freeze!"

"Did you say something?" asked the wolf.

"I'm casting spells," said the fox aloud. "Sit and wait, wait and sit, you'll have as many fish as you can wish."

And the wolf waited and shivered with cold. Just before dawn he wanted to pull the jug out of the water, but found he could not.

"Help me," the wolf howled to the fox. "I can't pull the jug out of the water!"

"Then you'll have to pull harder! It must be full of fish!" the fox advised him.

Just then, some women from the village came down to the river. When they caught sight of the wolf they began shouting, "A wolf, there's a wolf here!"

The men heard them and hurried over, some carrying sticks, others pitchforks. They set about beating the wolf, with shouts of, "So we've caught you at last, you thief! Now we'll pay you back for stealing our lambs and worrying our sheep and calves!"

The men laid on one blow after another and the wolf tugged this way and that. At last he managed to pull his tail out of the ice, and he limped off into the forest as fast as he could.

152

The fox lost no time, she slipped into the nearest cottage and poured porridge over her head. Then she, too, ran off into the forest. She caught up with the wolf and wailed,

"Oh me, oh my! We really did get a hiding this time!"

"What do you mean?" howled the wolf. "I got the beating and you're doing the wailing!"

"Take a better look at me, brother wolf! My legs are giving way under me!" the fox groaned. "They beat me so hard that my brains have run out. And all because you had to have fish for dinner! How am I to drag myself home like this?"

The wolf began to feel sorry for the fox. He sighed and said, "What am I to do with you? Jump on my back, I'll carry you."

That was just what the fox had been waiting for. In the twinkle of an eye she was up on the wolf's back, riding him like a horse.

The wolf dragged himself along the forest path, groaning under the burden. And the fox on his back chanted, "The beaten bears the unbeaten, the dull-witted, the quick-witted . . ."

"What's that you're chanting?" the wolf was curious to know.

"Nothing in particular, I'm just muttering to myself to take my mind off the pain in my head," the fox replied.

The wolf carried the fox home, right to her doorstep. She scampered around her den and after a while peeped out and laughed.

"You *are* stupid, you really are! Have you ever seen anyone catch fish in a jug? You must be a dimwit and no mistake about it if you can't tell the difference between brains and porridge! And it was you who got the beating, but you who carried me all the way home!"

The wolf became angry, "What do you mean by saying I'm stupid?" He pounced on the fox and caught her by the paw. But the fox went on taunting him,

"You are a stupid, stupid wolf – you can't even tell the difference between a root and a paw!"

The wolf let go of the fox's paw and caught hold of a root in the den. He pulled and pulled until he tore it up, at which point he fell backwards and rolled down the slope. He rolled over and over and over, and maybe he is still rolling to this very day unless a tree stump has stopped his fall.

Why monkeys
don't build houses

In the jungle there lived a group of monkeys. One day one of them left the others and ran off deeper into the jungle. On the way back she was caught in a shower of rain. The monkey could not understand what was happening. She was still very young and she had never seen rain before.

"What's this strange thing?" she muttered to herself. "The water is down in the lake. If I want to have a bath, I must go there. But now it's falling from above. I didn't jump into it, but I'm wet through."

She hid among the branches and when it stopped raining she continued on her way. Soon she met a tortoise. She told him all about what she had suffered and the tortoise laughed.

"That was rain falling from the sky. The sun sucks up water from the lake with its rays, stores it in the clouds and when it has too much, lets it fall back to earth again."

"How can I protect myself from the rain?" grumbled the monkey. "I don't like it when water keeps pouring over my head and down my back."

"Build a house. That will shelter you from the rain, from the sun and from the cold, too," said the tortoise, and went on his way. The monkey ran up a banana tree where some monkeys were feasting and called out,

"Sister monkeys, let's build a house. When it's ready we won't get wet or feel the cold!"

"Let's build one, let's build one!" shrieked the monkeys enthusiastically. "And not just an ordinary one in a tree, but one like people have, on the ground!"

They chattered and planned and planned and chattered until they were sent scattering by the rain. They hid wherever they could, keeping quiet until the rain had stopped. When they had got together again, they shrieked,

"We're not going to suffer like that any more. In the morning, as soon as the sun rises, we'll begin to build a house. It's too late to start today."

"Too late, much too late!" shrieked the little monkey. "Let's go and see what's new in the jungle!"

And off they ran to feast on the bananas in the banana tree. Then they went to see whether the oranges were ripe yet and what was new beside the lake. They swung through the trees and played until evening came.

In the morning, as soon as day broke, they met on a thick branch and decided,

"First we'll have breakfast, then we'll begin to build! There's time enough before evening comes!"

The group ran off to the banana tree and from there they went to see whether the dates and figs were getting ripe and finally they felt like bathing in the lake.

After their bath some of the monkeys warmed themselves in the sun, others jumped from branch to branch and called out,

"Let's rest for a while. Then we'll build our house."

They rested and rested, and then suddenly one of them exclaimed,

157

"Sisters, it's already evening! When are we going to start building?"

And another answered,

"It's not worth starting now. Let's play for a while instead!"

The other monkeys looked up at the sky and saw that the sun would soon be setting. They shrieked,

"It really is evening! How quickly the day has gone! What a good thing it didn't rain! We'll start building in the morning!"

They chattered on for a while and then scattered, each to her own branch.

That night it rained. In the morning the monkeys, numbed and wet through, gathered together groaning,

"We're wet through from head to tail! From head to tail we're numb with cold. First we must get dry and warm ourselves in the sun, then we'll begin to build a house."

As soon as the first rays of the sun appeared, they stretched themselves out on the rocks, and when they had dried out, they shrieked that they were hungry and ran off into the jungle to look for food. They ran here and there and everywhere and by the time they had remembered what they had planned to do, it was evening again.

And so it goes on to this very day. Many years have passed since that time, but monkeys have no houses. They warm themselves in the sun, get wet in the rain and keep promising themselves,

"Tomorrow we really will begin to build a house! We are not going to put up with this any more! As soon as the sun comes out, we'll set to work!"

But when the sun comes out, they run off to find some breakfast, then they look to see what's new in the jungle, and the process starts over and over again.

The man and the dog

There was once a dog. He lived in the forest. Because he felt lonely, he decided to look for a friend. On his way through the forest, he met a rabbit.

"You know what, rabbit? Let's live together!"

"All right," said the rabbit.

Evening came and they went to bed. In the night the dog barked. The rabbit woke up in fright and said, "Don't bark! The wolf will come and eat us up."

The dog thought to himself, "That's a fine friend I've found, scared stiff. I'd rather live with the wolf, he's sure not to be afraid of anyone."

He set out to find the wolf. Who knows how long he had to look, but in the end he found him.

"You know what, wolf?" he said to him. "Let's live together!"

"Why not? Let's!"

Evening came and they lay down to rest. The wolf fell asleep at once. At midnight the dog began to bark. The wolf woke up in alarm and hushed the dog, "For heaven's sake don't bark! The bear will hear us! He'll come and eat us up!"

The dog thought to himself, "The wolf isn't brave either, he's afraid of the bear. I'd rather live with the bear in that case."

He set off into the forest to find the bear. Who knows how long he had to look, but in the end he found him. He said to him, "Listen, bear, let's live together, the two of us!"

"Why not?" said the bear.

When it got dark, they lay down to rest. The bear was soon fast asleep. It was exactly midnight when the dog began to bark. The bear woke up in alarm. "Why are you barking? The man will hear you! He'll come and kill us!"

The dog thought to himself, "Who would have thought it? The bear is afraid, too. That's no friend for me! It'll be the man that's afraid of no one."

He ran off to look for the man.

Who knows how long he had to look, but in the end he found him. He was walking through the forest, hunting. The dog said to him, "Let's live together, the two of us."

"Why not?" said the man.

He took the dog to his home. Evening came. The man went to bed and fell asleep at once.

At exactly midnight the dog began to bark. The man woke up, but he showed no sign of fear. He said to the dog, "If you're hungry, have something to eat, but there's no need to wake me up."

The dog saw that the man was afraid of no one and decided to live on with him. And he still lives with him to this very day.

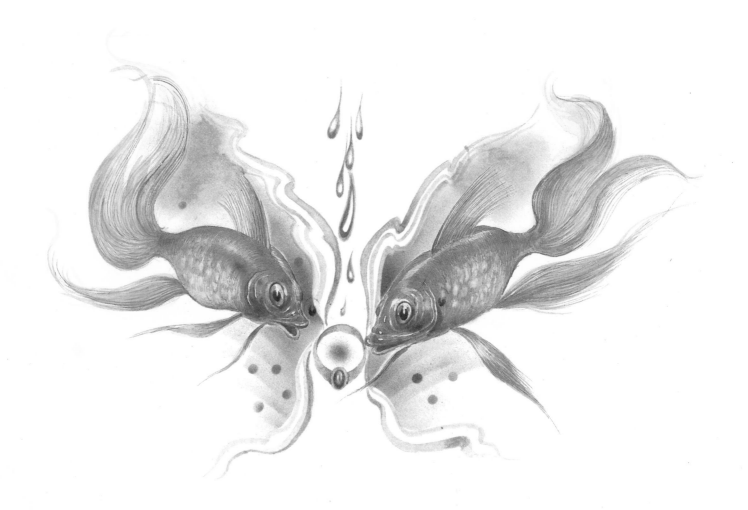